THE CASE OF THE
Mysterious
Madam

A GILDED AGE HISTORICAL COZY MYSTERY

ELISE M. STONE

This book is a work of fiction. Characters, names, places, and incidents in this novel are either the products of the imagination or are used fictitiously. Any resemblance to actual events or people, either living or dead, is entirely coincidental.

The Case of the Mysterious Madam

Copyright © 2020 Elise M. Stone

Cover designed by Shayne K. of Wicked Good Book Covers

All rights reserved. No part of this book may be reproduced, stored in a retrieval system, or transmitted in any form or by any means—electronic, mechanical, photocopying, or otherwise—without permission in writing from the copyright owner, except by a reviewer, who may quote brief passages in a review.

Published by Civano Press

Tucson, AZ

Copyright © 2020 Elise M. Stone
All rights reserved.
ISBN 9798639616549

CHAPTER 1

KATIE SULLIVAN LEANED against the bar that ran the length of the wall, surveying the action. One of two gambling rooms in the Seaview Hotel, she found Golden Chances a congenial place to approach potential clients. The din of conversation almost drowned out the plinking of a piano a few feet away, but Katie thought she recognized the song as one by vaudeville star George M. Cohan. The combination of music and chatter made it impossible to hear anything spoken more than six inches away from your ear. But Katie wasn't talking at the moment, so she didn't mind. Supporting her weight on her elbows, Katie stopped her scan at a table directly in front of her on the opposite side of the room.

It looked like Ranson Payne, chairman of the Board of Selectman, had himself another victim. Three of the other players were regulars, cronies of Payne who often sat down for a friendly game of poker of an evening. But the fourth was a newcomer, someone Katie hadn't seen in town before. There were always strangers in Whitby in the summer, but for some reason this one drew her attention. The middle-aged man wore a brown herringbone sack coat with a white shirt and tie. He'd already loosened his tie.

Despite the cooling sea breeze that came off the Atlantic Ocean in the evenings and blew through the open windows, his forehead shone with a sheen of perspiration in the light of the new electric chandeliers overhead. Katie preferred the old gaslit ones herself. They provided shadowed corners where you could talk privately, often essential in her line of work. The bright lighting seemed to discourage potential customers from speaking to her, afraid someone would notice them negotiating with the madam of the Honey House. But the patrons of the luxury hotels in Whitby expected such modern fixtures, and so electricity had been brought to this part of town.

The stranger's eyes narrowed as he stared at his cards. He had an intriguing air about him. While his dark beard and mustache were neatly trimmed, he wore his hair considerably longer than a gentleman would, with the ends a good inch below his collar. It gave him a rakish look.

A small pile of cash was stacked in front of him. From the size of the pile in the middle, Katie could only assume he'd contributed substantially to Payne's coming win. While the newcomer contemplated his next move, one of the waiters arrived at the table with a tray filled with drinks. He put a glass next to each one of the card players—except the stranger, who waved him off.

"Tony," she called out as the waiter came toward the bar to refill his tray. The young man filled out his black suit nicely, and

The Case of the Mysterious Madam

Katie knew from experience most of that wasn't from the revolver in the shoulder holster under his jacket. The crowd in the gambling room could get rowdy, and waiters were often hired as much for their fighting ability as their serving skills.

Tony detoured from his target and beelined toward her. "Good evening, Mrs. Sullivan. What can I do for you?"

"Who's the new sucker?" She indicated the stranger with a tilt of her chin.

Tony turned to see who she was asking about. His eyes widened with surprise, then he smiled at her. "Don't you know?"

Katie shifted her weight so she was no longer leaning on the bar and gave the young man a steely stare. "If I knew, would I be asking you?"

"Well, I thought you would have seen him in the papers. That's Titus Strong, the lawyer."

Katie gave the stranger a closer look. Now that Tony had identified him, he was unmistakable, if you ignored the shaggy hair and beard. He'd been in the Boston papers often enough over the last few weeks, usually posed next to his celebrity client, Richard Davenport. Davenport had been found standing over the body of his dead wife, a wife it was rumored he didn't get along with. Despite almost incontrovertible evidence to the contrary, Strong had gotten a not-guilty verdict. As always, money talked, whether in Boston or in Whitby.

"Anything else, Mrs. Sullivan?"

Katie shook her head without altering the direction of her gaze. "No, thanks."

Strong pushed his remaining cash into the center of the table, then showed his cards. With a knowing smile, Payne spread his hand on the table, then gathered in the pot. Strong rose to his feet, and after a word or two, left the table and headed in Katie's direction.

Katie gave him her welcoming-but-not-too-interested look as he approached the bar. Losers could often do with some consolation from one of her girls. She wondered if Titus Strong was one of those losers.

It wasn't hard to figure out the occupation of the woman with the long red hair and the emerald green gown. The gold brocade running down the front and around the hem was too ostentatious for a gentlewoman. Titus nodded, then turned his attention to the bartender, who hurried to serve him.

"Root beer," Strong said.

The bartender pulled a bottle of Hires from under the bar. Moisture fogged the sides of the glass and dripped down in rivulets to form a puddle around the base. It must have been sitting in a container of ice, a precious commodity in summer, but one which was expected in a hotel like the Seaview. The bartender wiped off the wet, poured half of its contents into a glass which he placed in front of the lawyer, then hurried off to serve another customer.

"I'd think you'd need something stronger." The woman's voice held no emotion. An observation, not a judgment.

Strong took a sip of his drink, then turned toward her. On closer look, tiny wrinkles around her eyes and mouth gave away her age, a greater number than he'd first assumed. "This is strong enough for me."

She took a long look at him, her eyes, emerald green to match her gown, sizing him up for her next line. He waited for what he knew was coming.

"Perhaps you'd like a different kind of comfort. Something a little more personal and feminine." Her voice purred seductively.

He shook his head. "No, thank you." He hadn't been wrong about her occupation.

Strong took another drink from his glass, this one longer, leaving only a small amount of the soft drink in the bottom. He wondered if she'd continue to pursue that line of conversation or, as he hoped, move on to another potential customer.

"Most men don't take a loss like the one you suffered so calmly."

He felt the blood rise in his face as his body tensed. He forced himself to take a few slow, deep breaths. "It happens. It's harder to read a man when you can't see his eyes."

"The glasses," she said.

"Right. Not only are the lenses almost black, the metal mesh on the sides hides whether his eyes are looking at his cards, or you, or another player, or anything else."

She must have noticed his perplexed expression. "Many albinos have light-sensitive eyes. It's the same lack of pigment that makes his hair and skin so pale."

Ah, that explained it then. He should have realized. But he hadn't. It was a sign of how distracted he'd been throughout the game. That wasn't at all like him. Usually he maintained a rapier focus on his opponent, whether at the card table or in the courtroom. This time his anger was more at himself than at the albino. Through clenched teeth, he said, "I know he was cheating, but I'm not sure how. I kept watching for him to manipulate his cards in some way, or perhaps have one up his sleeve, but either he's a magician, or he was winning legitimately."

"Ranson Payne doesn't lose in his town."

Strong refilled his glass from the bottle, then downed it in one swift movement. He could still feel the anger boiling inside of him; the heat of it spread through his body. He didn't like it when anger threatened his self-control. "It's too warm in here. I'm going to take a walk on the boardwalk."

"Would you like some company?" the woman asked.

Strong was going to say no, but he realized he wouldn't have told her where he was going unless he wanted her to go with him. *To blazes with it.* His wife was miles away, and she probably wouldn't care anyway as long as he showed up to escort her to the next society function. "Why not?"

He almost offered her his arm, but then realized that might be going too far. He headed for the door that led out to the beach, slowing his pace just enough to make sure she was beside him.

After a few steps, the din of the gambling room had given way to the soft sound of the surf and the whisper of the onshore breeze. The air smelled of salt and seaweed. It cooled Strong's face, and the rhythmic pounding of the waves soothed his anger.

Gaslights on both sides of the boardwalk lit their way, guiding the two of them on their stroll parallel to the beach. Once they were a sufficient distance from the hotel, Titus asked, "What did you mean by 'Ranson Payne doesn't lose in *his* town'?"

The wind blew her hair into a merlot-colored nimbus. She

raised a hand to brush it back from her face. "You've never been to Whitby before then?"

He shook his head.

"Payne is chairman of the Board of Selectmen. He and his friends control the liquor licenses, and that means they control most of the hotels and restaurants in town. They also control who gets to pave the streets, run the ferries and streetcars, and own beach property."

The gaslights that had lined the boardwalk to this point suddenly ended, pitching them into the darkness of a moonless night.

"And you're saying those licenses and permits and services aren't given out on merit."

She barked a laugh, answering his question. "They're more often sold to the highest bidder, with the bulk of the bid going into Payne's pockets."

"So how was he winning all those hands? Do you know his method?"

She stared down at her feet as she walked rather than looking at him. It bothered him. He wanted to look in her eyes, eyes which caught the starlight and reflected it back at him. It was the one way you could tell if someone was lying or not.

"*He* wasn't cheating," she said in a soft voice. "The dealer does it for him."

"Huh." He hadn't considered that option.

She cut toward the ocean and leaned on the railing of the boardwalk. Facing into the wind, her hair blew straight back. He was obsessed with that hair. He'd have to be careful he didn't become obsessed with her. He joined her and rested a foot on the lower rail. "My name is Titus Strong."

"I know," she said.

He wondered why she didn't volunteer the information an introduction usually prompted. "I don't know your name, though. Who are you?"

She turned her head and fixed her eyes on his, locking his gaze to hers as surely as if she'd used a padlock. "Katie Sullivan. I own the Honey House."

Her heart was beating stronger than she'd believed possible. She wondered if he'd understood her. Would he walk away in a huff after learning who she really was? You'd think, after all these years, what people thought wouldn't matter to her. But in this case, it did.

"An apt name." He said it as if she'd told him her name was Ann Smith and she sold jam for a living.

"You do know what the Honey House is?"

"I think I do," he said dryly.

Who was this Titus Strong? Most men would either be shocked and run from her or follow up with some salacious comment that usually ended with a request to get it free. Titus Strong did neither.

"What brings you to Whitby?" she asked. "Other than the poker games, that is."

A waning crescent moon rose over the ocean. The waves glittered as moonbeams caught the gently tumbling surf.

His face turned pensive. "I needed a break after the Davenport trial."

"That must have been a stressful situation, having a client who could be hanged if you didn't get him off." She wasn't sure that wouldn't have been the better option. From what she'd heard of the case, Davenport deserved the gallows.

Strong took his foot off the railing and stood with his feet spread apart, a stance that conveyed stability and strength. He jammed his hands in his pockets, then spoke. "It *was* stressful, but not because he might have been hanged. No, the stress came because I did my best to get him off, when I would have preferred to see him swing."

She was struck by his honesty. Titus Strong was definitely a different kind of man. "Couldn't you have refused to represent him?"

"Let's keep walking," he said as he suited his action to his words. His twitchy movements said he was still agitated, whether from the loss at poker or the Davenport trial, Katie couldn't tell.

After a few minutes, he spoke again. "Boston isn't so different from Whitby. The people in power control the game. If I'd refused the case, I most likely wouldn't have gotten another one like it." He grimaced. "I'd be relegated to bailing drunks out of jail at midnight and…"

He'd trailed off rather than say the next part, so Katie said it for him. "And defending women like me."

Strong nodded. The tips of his ears turned red. "I mean no disrespect."

Katie laughed. "That would be a first."

When his eyes widened, she added, "I am what I am. There are very few ways a woman can make a living, especially in a town like Whitby. I'm not embarrassed about it, nor ashamed. You shouldn't be, either."

"I'm not, exactly." He stopped as if reconsidering. Then he looked at her and smiled. "Well, maybe just a little."

"Most men are. But I have a feeling you're different from most men. That's why defending Richard Davenport bothers you. The shysters I've known would be all too happy to pocket the money and forget about whether what they were doing was right or wrong."

"I can't disagree with you." They'd reached the end of the boardwalk, the marker where the public beaches used by guests of the hotels and day-trippers gave way to the summer cottages of the rich. The silhouettes of the three-storied structures blocked out a good part of the sky. "We should turn back."

An obvious statement, but one that had to be made. The two of them strolled back to the Seaview Hotel. Mostly they were silent. Katie wondered about this intriguing man who was at ease with both the wealthy and a woman like herself. It would probably be too much to hope they might become friends.

When they reached the entrance to the hotel, Strong said, "I've enjoyed our walk together tonight. Thank you for filling me in on Payne." For a moment, a shadow crossed his face as if he were considering something. "Perhaps we might do this again sometime."

"I'd like that," she said.

CHAPTER 2

Titus was awakened from a deep sleep by the sounds of shouting—a drunken man, a strident woman—coming from outside his door. A scream had him leaping from his bed and charging barefoot into the hallway.

He'd been right about the drunken man. In his mid-fifties, with a weather-worn face and a bulbous nose, the wiry figure had a death grip on the mutton sleeve of a young woman who struggled to escape his grasp and flee into the room behind her. Her red dress was torn down the front, exposing the roundness of her breasts beneath the low-cut camisole.

Facing the man was Katie Sullivan, a nickel-plated, two-barreled derringer pointed at the drunk.

"Let go of her, Cooper," Mrs. Sullivan said with menace in her eyes.

"Awww, Katie. You wouldn't interfere with a bit o' fun, would you?"

Katie's grip on the gun tightened. "I told you to let go of her."

Titus wasn't sure what he should do. He longed to leap to Mrs. Sullivan's aid, but the situation was too tense, and she might pull the trigger if he did. A whimper came from the girl as the drunk tugged on her arm. The drunk bent to kiss her.

"Mr. Cooper." Titus used the most authoritative voice he could muster, the one he usually reserved for cross-examination. "I'd recommend you do as the lady asked."

The drunk swiveled in Strong's direction, peered at him with bleary eyes. "Who be you?"

"A man who won't stand for a lady being abused."

"What lady?"

A number of other people had opened their doors to see what all the commotion was about: a man with a high forehead, an elderly couple who looked frightened, one of the men Strong had played poker with last evening. He seemed to remember the poker player's name was Hinkle.

Footsteps thudded up the stairs at the end of the hall before Titus could respond. Two men appeared and hurried toward the disturbance. Well, the younger one hurried. He wore a uniform, complete with a domed custodian helmet bearing a shiny shield on the front. He had an athletic build. Uncertainty tightened his face. He stopped a few feet away, evaluating the situation. Behind him, a bulkier, older man in a suit huffed and puffed as he caught up, too out of breath to speak.

"What do we have here?" the police officer asked.

Mrs. Sullivan, still keeping the derringer pointed at Cooper, said, "Nate here tried to rape Emily. I heard her screaming and stopped him."

"Is that true, Emily?" the policeman asked.

Emily, a tear rolling down her cheek, nodded.

"Now, now," the fat man in the suit said. "Let's not get carried away."

Lava flowed through Strong's veins as a fiery anger flooded through him. A nerve twitched in his clenched jaw. *Who was that man?*

Mrs. Sullivan lowered the hand holding the gun and swirled in the fat man's direction. Her hands and voice were trembling. "Rape is not 'getting carried away', Chief."

"Katie, Katie." The man was shaking his head. "What we have here is theft. So far. I think we should give Nate a chance to complete his transaction." He addressed the drunk. "Now, if you'll let go of Emily and pay up, we'll call it square."

Nate released the girl and opened his mouth to speak.

Assuming what the answer would be, the chief turned to speak to the madam. "Okay, Katie?"

Before Mrs. Sullivan could respond, Nate Cooper stammered, "I... uh... don't have any muh-ney... Chief."

With a smile and a wink, the chief said, "You will in a few days, Nate. I'm sure Emily would be willing to put your transaction on account until then."

Katie was breathing hard. Without the support of the police, Titus wasn't sure she could insist on an arrest. He wondered if he ought to threaten civil charges, but from what he'd heard so far of the way Whitby was run, it wouldn't make any difference. Besides, he'd been hoping to keep a low profile on his vacation. No, better to let Mrs. Sullivan handle this herself.

"Okay, Katie?" the chief repeated.

Katie nodded reluctantly.

"There, you see? Everything's fine." The chief turned toward the young officer. "I think we can let these good people go back to bed now."

The officer looked unsure, but he wasn't about to challenge the chief, either. Strong wondered what—or who—stood behind the power the chief wielded. He had a feeling it was Ranson Payne.

"Let's go, Tim." The chief turned on his heel and led the way back down the hall. The elderly couple retreated and closed the door to their room.

Once the police were out of earshot, Mrs. Sullivan put her hands on her hips and glared at the drunk. "This isn't the end of this, Cooper. You're going to pay for what you did, and I don't mean the pittance you'll come up with to give to Emily."

Cooper cowered, then slunk away down the hall. Mrs. Sullivan slid her arm around the girl and coaxed her back inside her hotel room as she murmured comforting words.

Strong looked at the other two men. The expression of the one with the high forehead conveyed nothing. The poker player shrugged, then retreated into his room, as did Titus.

The whole incident disturbed him. This was the second time tonight the ugly underbelly of Whitby had exposed itself. He'd thought Whitby was a happy place, a place where you could spend a day in the sun and a night in the gambling rooms enjoying yourself. He'd hoped to recuperate from the intensity of the trial in Boston. But it seemed as if Whitby had its own intensity, and not of the good kind.

Chapter 3

Despite the interrupted sleep—or maybe because of it, Titus woke up early. He approached the dining room, but a waiter in a black jacket and stiffly starched white shirt intercepted him before he reached it.

"I'm sorry, sir, but we're not serving breakfast yet."

"That's all right," Titus said. "But could I get a cup of coffee? And perhaps a newspaper?"

"I might be able to arrange that. Please follow me."

The empty dining room seemed cavernous without the usual complement of diners at the white linen-covered tables laid out in china, crystal, and silver. The waiter showed him to a place not too far from the door.

"Might I sit near the windows? I'd prefer to look over the ocean."

"Of course, sir." The waiter led Titus to a second table. "Will this do?"

"This one will be fine." Titus seated himself and spread his napkin on his lap while the waiter hurried off for his coffee. The waves, which had been gentle since Titus had arrived in Whitby, today seemed more agitated, with some sporting caps of white foam.

A man walked his dog along the beach. The pup darted in and out of the surf, shaking himself dry each time he left the water. Every once in a while, the man would throw a stick for the dog to retrieve. The dog was happy to oblige, running after the stick and, from the movements of his jaw, barking loudly in his pursuit. The scene made Titus smile. He hadn't had a dog since he moved to Boston. His wife didn't like animals, and he didn't have the time to properly care for one.

The waiter soon returned with a tray that held not only a cup of coffee and a newspaper, but a small plate of pastries as well. Titus's mouth watered at the sight of them. He smiled up at the waiter who, like all good waiters, remained impassive.

"Shall I put this on your bill, sir?"

"Yes, thank you. And thank you for the pastries."

Titus put a drop of cream in his coffee and eagerly took a sip. He almost sighed aloud. Coffee was the nectar of the gods, particularly the first cup in the morning. The tenth cup at eight at night from a pot that was brewed in the afternoon was more like tar, but it had been the rare day when he'd turned down even one of those.

He picked up a strawberry tart and unfolded the paper to browse the headlines. They were a little different from what he'd find in a Boston paper. The lead story was about the Fourth of July celebrations in town, including a band concert and a clambake put on by the Oddfellows. It sounded like quite the time. At least he'd have something to do over the holiday.

Once he finished his coffee and his tart, a walk near the water sounded like just the thing he needed. He signed the bill that the waiter had unobtrusively dropped off while he was eating and left the restaurant.

Rather than walk along the ocean on the east side of the spit of land that comprised the town of Whitby, he thought he'd walk on the opposite, where the ferry from Boston had dropped him off a few days before. He wanted to take a look at the village. When he reached Mayfield Road, which formed the backbone of the peninsula, he turned right.

It was too early for any of the stores to be open, but he made a note of the bookstore and a restaurant named Jake's to explore some time in the future. He was trying to remember where the horse-drawn cab had turned onto Mayfield so he could follow the same route in reverse, when he came upon Steamboat Avenue. It didn't take a genius to surmise that this was the way to the ferry dock.

The first ferry of the day was disgorging its passengers, most of them families on a day trip to the beach. Titus stayed away from the crowd, skirting the area where the pickpockets plied their trade on the unsuspecting. He watched as a pair worked their artifice, one juggling a trio of rubber balls to distract a person, the other working his way around the backs of the spectators and lightly reaching inside their pockets as quickly as he could.

Titus shook his head and walked away, thinking to take a closer look at the Bay Royale Hotel, the most exclusive one in Whitby. The Bay Royale was built on a rise just past a small cove up ahead. Tall, leafy green trees stood in front of the façade, with a lawn forming a carpet in front of them. All he could see from here was the American flag that flew above a dormer on what he estimated was the third floor of the hotel.

Strolling by the marina which took up most of one side of the cove, Titus admired the yachts anchored at the small docks that jutted out perpendicular to the shoreline. His partnership in the law firm didn't allow for such a luxury… yet. Then he remembered why he was here instead of in Boston and wondered if he'd ever own a yacht. Or even a rowboat.

He was surprised when he reached another dock, this one running parallel to the shore, the boats tied up there not yachts at all. A sign overhead read Charter Fishing Trips.

A distinct New England accent filled with broad vowels and clipped consonants called out to him. "You ought to go fishing on this fine day."

CHAPTER 4

A BUCKET HAT shaded the weathered face of a man who had spent the better part of his life outdoors. Except for a chin covered in a short, white beard, creases mapped most of his face, and his cheekbones were highlighted in wind-chapped red.

"Why would that be?" Titus asked.

"Because you won't be able to tomorrow." The old fisherman glanced at the choppy water, then up at the sky. "Storm's comin' in."

Titus craned his neck to look up. Overhead the sky was a deep blue with no sign of a storm, but he'd take the man's word for it. Someone who made his living on the water was bound to know the signs of a storm better than a city man. The old fisherman also wore a sou'wester, whether for protection from the forecast rain or the splash of the sea, Titus didn't know.

"What does it cost?"

Surprised by the reasonableness of the price, Titus considered the offer. It was a little early to start losing money in the gambling room at the hotel, and he had no other plans for the day. He wasn't wearing one of his city suits, so he didn't care if it got wet. A little salt water wouldn't do much harm.

"All right. Count me in." He headed for the ladder hanging over the side of the boat.

The old fisherman reached out to give him a hand up onto the deck when he got to the top of the ladder. "My name's Joe Kelley and this is the sloop Arvilla. Welcome aboard!"

For a second, he considered making up a name, knowing his had been in the headlines not too long ago. But what had made him flee Boston was the need to be honest with himself, not the need to tell more lies. *I am who I am.* "Titus Strong."

Three other men, by their appearance also visitors who'd paid Kelley to go fishing, were sizing him up. None of them looked particularly surprised. None of them looked particularly interested, either. He stared pointedly at the one to his left.

"Owen Campbell," said the man with the walrus mustache and piercing blue eyes.

"Cyrus Lawson," said the middle one.

"Addison Slater," said the third.

Kelley regarded them with amusement. "Now that we've gotten that over with, would two of you fine gentlemen pull in the lines while I go raise the sail?"

"I'll do it," Titus said and jogged to the bow. A dock hand was untying the line. Finding the other end tied to a cleat, Titus grasped it and waited for the dock hand.

Kelley paused a minute. "Gentlemen, I need someone at the

stern if we're going to leave the dock."

Owen Campbell rose from his seat on the port side and headed toward the rear of the boat.

The dock hand tossed the line toward Titus, who started pulling it in. The man ran toward the stern to unleash that line. Meanwhile, Kelley raised a small sail at the front of the mast. The bow swung out away from the dock as the wind caught the jib. Campbell pulled in the stern line as the boat sailed out into the cove.

"Coil those lines on the deck," Kelley called as he raised the mainsail, then dashed to the tiller to steer the boat out into open water.

Titus did as he was told, then turned to face forward, enjoying the wind and the spray cooling his face on this warm July day. He couldn't believe what a lucky turn of events had brought him to this adventure. He'd only been looking for something to plan on doing in the future, and here he found himself taking part in the ultimate seaside experience.

He turned around when he felt the boat slowing down. Kelley had furled the mainsail and locked the tiller in some fashion. He dropped an anchor over the side, then ducked into the cabin, returning a moment later with a handful of fishing rods. Titus headed sternward to claim his.

As the men baited their hooks with chunks of fish from a bucket, Kelley gave them instructions. "If you'll stand along the port side and cast your lines into the water, you should be able to hook a bluefish or ten."

Titus followed the instructions, and the other three fishermen clustered around him.

"Not so close together! You chowder-headed land-lubbers

are gonna tangle your lines and hook one another." He shook his head at them as if they were five-year-olds on the first day of school.

"Salty, isn't he?" Campbell said in a barely audible voice from about four feet away.

"Colorful, I'd say," Titus replied.

"I'm surprised you've time to go on a fishing trip."

"What do you mean?"

"With your famous courtroom victory, I'd think you'd have more clients than you could handle."

Titus should have known what the man was referring to in the first place. He'd never get away from his infamous victory. "That might be so, but I'm not interested in the clients that are knocking on my office door right about now."

"Oh?"

Titus wasn't exactly sure what the tone of that one syllable meant. If anything, he'd have to call it curious. He'd rather direct the conversation away from himself. "How do you earn your living, if I might ask?"

"You might." Campbell was quiet for so long, Titus wondered if he wasn't going to answer the question. Finally, he said, "I'm a Pinkerton detective."

Now it was Titus's turn to be interested. "You don't say. I bet you have some fascinating stories you could tell."

The Pinkerton licked his lips. "There are some I'd prefer not to tell. Especially about Homestead." His face turned to granite.

So Campbell had been involved in that disaster. Andrew Carnegie had been determined to break the union that had won concessions after a bitter strike. He fired all the union members, but the result was all the other workers joined them. The Pinkertons had been called in to break up the strike, and a gun battle between the factions followed. In the end, the Pinkertons surrendered.

"It appears I'm not the only one seeking to escape from an unpleasant event in his recent past," Titus said.

At that moment Campbell's line started jumping, and the pole almost jerked out of his hand. Surprised by the strike, he pulled fiercely on the pole.

"Not that way, you bloody fool!" Kelley yelled. "Use the reel."

He charged across the deck so he'd be closer to Campbell, as if he thought the detective might not have heard him. If Strong was any judge, half the population of Whitby had heard his admonition, even though they were far from shore by now.

"That's it," Kelley said in a calmer voice. "Now let 'em run for a bit. You have to tire them out before they'll surrender totally." One side of his mouth quirked up. "Of course, bluefish don't often surrender *totally*."

Titus was enthralled by the battle and almost missed the tug on his own line. "Whoa!"

Kelley's head jerked up, and he quickly left Campbell's side to coach his next neophyte. More fish leapt out of the water, roiling it like a pot ready for a lobster boil. Soon all of the men were battling fish on their lines. Kelley was in his glory, hopping from one to the other with words of what Titus was sure he thought was sage advice.

The old fisherman dodged over to Campbell. "Time to reel him in."

The detective followed instructions, and soon a four-pound

bluefish was thrashing on the deck.

"Take the hook out," Kelley said. "Mind the teeth."

Campbell did as he was told. Kelley stepped in, knife in hand, and sliced behind the gills. "Gotta let 'em bleed." He repeated the process as the others reeled their bluefish in. They quickly baited their hooks again and cast them over the side. For twenty or thirty minutes, the men focused on catching fish. No more waiting idly and swapping stories.

Blood and fish guts soon covered the deck. The smell was... intense.

"Strong!" Kelley yelled, surprising Titus. "Get the ice chest from the cabin."

Titus ducked low to descend into the cabin, took a minute as his eyes adjusted to the dimness after the bright light of the sun reflecting off the water. He spied the chest and hefted it up the stairs. When he got back on deck, the men were washing the fish in the seawater. They tossed the clean ones in the chest full of ice as soon as he opened it, grinning and congratulating one another on their success.

"Catching bluefish is easy," Kelley said. "Damn fish are always hungry, even when they're full." He allowed a smile to tug at his lips. "But you did a good job for landlubbers."

When all the fish were cleaned and put on ice, Kelley raised the anchor, then headed for the tiller and turned the boat north. "Mind the boom," he said dryly when it swung across the boat, almost knocking Lawson overboard.

Titus thought the trip would be over now that they'd caught so many bluefish. In fact, he wondered what they'd do with them. Perhaps the others had rented one of the small beach houses for a time, but staying at a hotel, he had no use for raw fish.

"Now we're going to try to catch some real fish."

The shoreline was still visible on the starboard side, but it seemed to be getting farther away. A knob of land appeared through the haze, and the sails luffed as Kelley pulled on the tiller to go around it. As they got into open water, the gentle breeze changed to fitful gusts. The sloop bounced over the choppy sea, confirming Joe Kelley's forecast of rough weather.

Titus grasped the edge of the bench where he rested after their strenuous encounter with the bluefish. The others were seated nearby, Campbell next to him, Lawson and Slater farther down. Slater, who looked like a laborer in his not-quite shabby suit that stretched tightly over his muscular arms, spoke up.

"Hey, Kelley," he shouted over the wind. "What's this I hear about a pirate ship?"

Kelley turned the boat northeast. The sails caught the wind and swelled full and firm. "Some say there was one, some say there wasn't."

"Didn't it sink off the coast of Whitby?" Slater insisted. "And wasn't it filled with treasure chests of Spanish gold doubloons?"

"Might have." Kelley had lit a pipe after he'd finished gutting and storing the fish, and now he cupped the bowl as he drew in some smoke. Once he breathed it out, he pointed to the rocky coast nearby. "It's dangerous rounding the Point. Many ships have hit the rocks and sunk. Others landed on the sandbar off the beach in a storm."

A lighthouse with a small attached cottage came into view as they continued past the headland. Kelley pointed his pipestem at the lighthouse. "That's why the lighthouse was built. It helps. Some. But we still call that Shipwreck Point. In fact, folks who live here don't call the town Whitby. Some fancy pants land developer came up with the name to entice people from Boston to buy property he owned. Those who live here, the real residents of the town, why, we just call the whole thing Shipwreck Point."

It sounded ominous. "Surely, what with the lighthouse and all, there aren't shipwrecks nowadays," Titus said.

Kelley raised an eyebrow. "A lighthouse doesn't change the winds or the currents. Or make ship's captains any smarter. We still have a lifesaving crew to rescue people from ships that wreck off the coast."

Kelley fixed the tiller, got up, and lowered the mainsail, slowing the boat down considerably.

"But what about the treasure?" Slater persisted.

The old fisherman spat over the leeward side of the boat, then turned to face Slater. His nostrils flared as he took a breath and pointed at the ice chest. *"There's* your treasure. Wishing for Spanish gold isn't going to make you any richer. But there, there's something you can eat, something you can sell, a way to make a living for your family."

He was breathing heavily now and took a moment to calm himself. "And now, if you've learned anything I've taught you today, you'll have a chance to add to it. Grab your rods, you lubbers. Let's see if you can catch some stripers."

CHAPTER 5

STRONG PICKED UP his poker hand as a heavy rain pelted the windows and the wind whistled through a gap between the window and the frame. Kelley had been right about the storm. Shortly before supper, dark clouds had moved in off the ocean.

If the weather had kept Payne away from the poker table, Titus considered it a good sign. If it was something else, well, he'd take what luck came his way. He was hoping to win back at least half of what he'd lost last night. A flash of lightning and the crack of thunder presaged a flicker of the electric lights. He wondered if anyone had kept candles or lanterns after the electricity had been put in.

He looked at the cards he'd been dealt. Ace of spades, king of diamonds. An auspicious start. He fingered his coins as he considered his bet. He didn't get a chance to place it.

A man in oilskins dripping with rainwater burst through the

outside entrance to the gambling room and shouted, "There's a ship wrecked on the bar." He dashed back out the door.

It didn't take long for the gamblers to look at one another and come to a consensus. Most of them rose from their chairs and ran to follow the man in the rain gear. Strong, not sure what was going on, put down his hand and followed.

A crowd surged down the beach toward Shipwreck Point. Some carried ropes and life preservers, others blankets, and yet others were empty-handed, but racing along the shore with everyone else. Another bolt of lightning split the sky, and Strong looked out toward the water to see if he could spy the ship.

Maybe a hundred yards or so from him, he could make out the masts of a large ship, a schooner most likely from the size of her. The masts tilted toward the water, showing how it had foundered on the sandbar. Not sure what he could do to help, Strong took his time getting to where the rescuers were working.

The sound of a gun firing made him hurry his steps. A line now ran from a tripod set up on the beach out to the sinking ship. As Strong watched, a group of men rigged a pulley and another line to it, then finally a kind of basket with a life preserver around the top. They pulled on the rope, sending the device out to the ship. The storm and the dark made it too difficult to see exactly what happened at the other end, but in a few minutes, the basket returned with a person in it. There must have been holes in the bottom, because Strong could see the man's legs hanging beneath the basket.

In another flash of lightning, the sea boiled with objects in the heavy surf. It reminded Titus of the bluefish they'd caught this morning thrashing about in a frenzy, the ones he had gladly handed over to the old fisherman to sell. Then he realized what was thrashing wasn't fish, but people who had abandoned the schooner. Even as he watched, two or three boats launched into the surf, the men rowing furiously toward the survivors.

For some reason, Strong felt drawn to keep going toward the Point. His instincts were right. While most of those from the ship clustered around the area of the rescue device, there was a man flailing out where the waves broke a dozen yards from where Strong now stood. He waded into the water.

"Over here!" The man didn't seem to hear him at first, then turned in his direction. He struggled to swim toward Strong, but was too weak to make much progress. Pulling off his shoes and throwing off his jacket, Strong tossed them up on the beach, then took a deep breath and dove into the water. With powerful strokes he attempted to swim out to meet the tiring survivor. The tide was coming in, and swimming against it was like wrestling a leviathan. Several times Titus choked on a mouthful of salt water as the sea slapped him in the face.

When Titus finally reached the struggling man, he rolled over on his back and hooked an arm under the man's chin. With a powerful kick, he headed toward shore, stroking with one arm and making sure to keep the man's mouth above water with the other. He was out of breath by the time they reached shallow water where he could stand. The man he'd rescued struggled to his feet and breathed, "Thanks, mate."

A plump woman, skirt flapping in the breeze, ran up with a blanket. She quickly draped the blanket around the man's shoulders. "Let's get you under cover."

Strong took several deep breaths, recovering his strength. He was a fairly good swimmer, but swimming in calm water was a lot different than swimming in a storm. He wiped an arm across his face, a useless gesture as the rain soaked it as soon as his arm was out of the way.

He thought he saw someone else in the water and peered through the night. Yes! A woman, if the long blonde hair was any clue. He got ready to jump in the water again, when he realized she was swimming out to sea rather than in toward shore. She must be disoriented from her struggles.

"Halloooo!" he called. "Wrong way! Swim toward me!"

She kept going in the wrong direction. She must not be able to hear him over the roar of the surf. He tried yelling louder. "Over here!"

She stopped for a second and looked back over her shoulder.

"This way!" He waved his hands above his head.

He was thinking he'd need to dive in again when a lifeboat appeared close by. The team rowed toward her, the bow rising and dipping as it lurched over the storm-tossed waves. He watched as they pulled her over the side, relieved he wouldn't have to battle the ocean again. One of the men in the boat put a blanket around the woman. She seemed to be okay.

Strong turned to head back to the hotel. The young policeman from last night stood nearby, holding Titus's shoes and jacket.

"Good job," he said as he handed Titus his shoes. "Not many would be willing to jump in the water the way you did."

"It was the right thing to do," Titus said as he crammed his feet into his swollen leather oxfords. He held out his hand. "Titus Strong."

"Good to meet you, Mr. Strong," the policeman said as he shook the proffered hand. "Tim Kelley."

Titus bent over to tie his shoes, then stopped, caught by the name. He knew there were a lot of Kelleys in this world, but this seemed like too much of a coincidence. "You wouldn't happen to be any relation to Joseph Kelley, would you?"

Tim smiled. "He's my grandfather. Have you gone fishing with him then?"

Titus resumed tying his shoes. "This morning. I enjoyed it."

"That's good to hear." Tim Kelley handed him his jacket.

"He told us about the shipwrecks. I'm surprised this one happened, now that there's a lighthouse and everything." He turned toward the Point. The police officer turned with him. Strong's jaw dropped.

The light was out.

The two men looked at one another, then as if by mutual agreement, hotfooted it down the shore. The rain had let up, but the wind still blew strong off the ocean. He'd be freezing if he were standing still.

Once they reached the Point, the sandy shoreline gave way to gravelly ground. Titus veered toward the lighthouse, but Tim Kelley grabbed his sleeve and steered him toward the front door of the cottage. "This way."

Tim took the lead. When he reached the entrance to the cottage, he opened the door. Surprised that the door was unlocked, Titus followed him inside. The policeman came to a sudden stop. Titus had to pull up short in order not to run into him. An inch taller than Kelley, it was no problem for Titus to see over his shoulder.

They'd entered a cozy, if somewhat shabby, parlor. A couch

on the wall had been positioned opposite a redbrick fireplace, close enough to feel the heat in all its intensity when the fireplace was lit. At the moment, all that was left was ashes, with a section that glowed red each time the outside wind gusted through the open door. Mingled with the aroma of ashes, damp, and dust was the faint scent of roses. A painting of the lighthouse hung over the fireplace.

A chair, the cushion darker than its back, stood to the right. Much of the room was in disarray, as if someone had searched it. A stack of papers that must have been neatly piled on the desktop scattered like birds in the draft from the door. On a bookcase beside the desk, the books were lined up like soldiers on a parade ground on one shelf. An ordinary room in an ordinary cottage in a Massachusetts summer town, except for the disconnect between chaos and order.

He followed Kelley's gaze toward the middle of the floor. Part of him wished he hadn't looked. Sprawled on the carpet in front of the couch lay Nate Cooper, a blossom of red in the center of his chest.

Beside him was a nickel-plated, two-barreled, pearl-handled derringer.

Chapter 6

"Stay here while I check the building," Officer Kelley ordered as he drew his pistol.

Strong did as he was told. He had no desire to run into the murderer, even though without the derringer he was most likely unarmed now. He heard doors opening and closing as Kelley checked each room, then an echo of footsteps on wooden planks that first faded away and then got louder.

"All clear," Officer Kelley said after he returned from making sure the killer was no longer present. He holstered his pistol. "Not much doubt about the cause of death,"

"No, not much." A weight had settled in the middle of Strong's chest while he awaited the policeman's return. He recognized the derringer. He wondered if Tim Kelley did.

The young Irishman cocked his head and gave Strong a thoughtful look.

"What is it?" Titus asked.

Tim Kelley shifted his weight. "I should go get Chief Morgan and inform the funeral home to be ready to pick up the body. But I don't want to leave the crime scene unsupervised. Would you mind staying and making sure no one else comes in?"

Titus couldn't believe his luck. He'd been wondering how he could take a closer look at things, but been afraid the policeman would prevent him from doing that. "Not at all. I doubt there will be many people coming out this way, what with the weather and everything."

"Thanks. I'll be back as soon as I can."

Kelley headed back the way they'd come. Titus kneeled down beside the body. He could see the hole where the bullet had entered Cooper, the center of a flower whose bloody petals flowed over the man's chest. Whoever killed him must have been a good shot. Or stood very close to his victim when he fired. Titus noticed he'd avoided using the feminine pronoun. He couldn't believe Katie Sullivan, no matter how angry she'd been over the abuse of one of her girls, would have killed the man. Or maybe it was that he didn't want to believe the woman was a murderer.

Now that he had a closer view, he could see another hole near the shoulder in the lighthouse keeper's jacket. This wound hadn't bled nearly as much as the other. It appeared whoever had murdered Nate Cooper had needed two shots, one from each cylinder of the derringer, to do the deed.

Titus glanced at the gun. It surprised him that the killer had left it behind. It was almost too convenient that the murder weapon remained for the police to collect. Too convenient that it pointed to a suspect.

A shaft of moonlight broke through the storm clouds and shone through a nearby window, glinting off some bit of something a few feet away. Curious, Titus got up to see what it was. He bent over and found a pie-shaped piece of silver. He picked it up to examine it more closely. From the grooved edges and the engraved surface, Titus inferred it was part of a coin. He could discern the tips of a crown on the point of the wedge. The letters S-P-A were clearly legible, with the serif beside them suggesting the bottom of a fourth letter.

Titus's eyes widened. He couldn't be sure, but a recollection of a sketch he'd seen in a history book while at law school suggested this was a Spanish piece-of-eight. There would be seven other wedges that would make up the full coin. Could the story of the pirate treasure be true? Had Cooper found its remains on the rocky shore of Shipwreck Point? And, if he had, had someone else wanted it badly enough to kill for?

He absentmindedly dropped the artifact in his pocket as he gave the room a closer look. There was something in the fireplace other than the ashes. He crossed the room and bent down to examine it. The corner of a piece of stationery was all that remained of a letter. The pastel color of the paper and the careful handwriting told him it had been written by a woman. He had no idea what Katie Sullivan's handwriting looked like. He was tempted to snatch the remnant out of the fireplace, but he knew it could be evidence, so left it where it was.

He decided to take a cursory look through the keeper's cottage while he waited. There wasn't much to see. Like most men who lived alone, Nate Cooper had been casual about housekeeping. Worn clothing was draped over a chair in the bedroom. The smell of boiled cabbage lingered in the kitchen, where a few dirty dishes sat in the sink. A combination utility room and office held a coal furnace and a shelf full of official looking books. Titus opened the door at the far end of this room.

He saw a wooden tunnel leading toward the lighthouse. Titus supposed it wasn't actually a tunnel, since it was above ground, but the tight quarters felt like one. The invention must have been a necessity in weather like tonight, even more so when a winter gale blew across the spit of land that stuck out into the ocean. The keeper wouldn't need to go out into it to pass from the house to the lighthouse spire. The rough wooden floor, more like a boardwalk than a real floor, explained the strange sounds he'd heard when Officer Kelley had gone through the premises.

He was just about to enter the tunnel when he heard heavy footsteps pounding outside. They grew louder, and he knew he didn't have time to explore further. Titus hurried to return to the sitting room. He opened the door to see who was coming.

"Who's out there?" he called out.

"It's me, Mr. Strong," Tim Kelley yelled.

The policeman soon arrived, followed by the corpulent police chief and another man whom Titus assumed was from the funeral home. Either that, or he was another policeman, but Titus wasn't sure the tiny town of Whitby had that large a police force.

"You can go now," Chief Morgan said.

"I'd prefer to stay," Strong replied.

The chief sized him up, then conceded. "Stay out of the way, then, while we do our work."

Strong nodded and took a place next to the door where he

could observe the whole room.

"Two shots," Morgan said after looking at the body. "Check the gun, see if both chambers are empty."

Tim Kelley picked up the gun. There was a click and then Kelley tilted the barrels down. He peered into them. "Empty." Then he sniffed the gun. "It's been fired recently."

Morgan laughed. "No surprise there." He slid a hand inside his jacket and scratched his massive belly while he looked thoughtful. "I think we can eliminate half the population of Shipwreck Point. Probably more than half. That's not a man's weapon."

Strong's heart thudded in his chest.

The chief focused on Tim Kelley. "How many women do you know who carry a derringer?"

It was the young officer's turn to look thoughtful. "None, as a matter of fact."

Was Tim Kelley lying? Or did he honestly not know that Katie Sullivan owned that gun? It would be useful to know if Kelley was protecting the woman, but he'd have to wait for a time when Chief Morgan wasn't around. Preferably a time when someone else had revealed the owner of the derringer. Strong wished he could make himself invisible. It didn't work.

"How about you?" Morgan asked him. "Do you have any idea who the gun belongs to?"

"I'm just a visitor here," Strong said. "I haven't had a chance to meet many people, especially not many women." He hoped Morgan wouldn't notice that he'd not actually answered the question.

The sound of horses' hooves on the road outside interrupted their conversation. The third man, who had been standing in the doorway, hat in hand, spoke up. "That's my man with the hearse. Is it okay if we remove the body now? I'd like to get back to my bed before the sun comes up."

Morgan looked at Kelley. "Anything else you want to look for?"

Kelley shook his head.

"You can take him away."

The man from the funeral home went outside for a minute, then returned with a second man and a stretcher. They loaded Cooper on the stretcher and left the cottage.

"Quite a mess in here," Chief Morgan said. "I wonder if she found what she was looking for."

"Do you want me to take a look around?" Tim Kelley asked as he scanned the room.

Morgan did the same, which caused him to spy Strong leaning against the wall. "Are you still here?"

"I didn't see any reason to go," Strong replied.

"I would have thought you'd opt for a ride back with the hearse. It's a long walk back into town."

"To be honest, I didn't think of it. I was too interested in observing your investigation of the crime scene."

"Who are you, anyway?" Morgan glared at him.

"My name is Titus Strong."

"You say that like it should mean something to me."

Tim Kelley interrupted. "It should. Don't you remember? Titus Strong is the lawyer who defended Richard Davenport in that murder trial in Boston last month."

Morgan pursed his lips and was still for a minute. Strong knew what he was thinking. He was thinking that the chief of police didn't want a criminal defense attorney observing his methods. He might see too much, know too much. Not that Strong was going to be part of whatever trial might result following the investigation of the homicide. But he might, as a professional courtesy, consult with the lawyer who did defend the suspected killer.

"You should leave." The chief's tone brooked no disagreement, and Titus thought it would probably be a bad idea to get on the chief's bad side.

"Very well, then," Titus said, and headed toward the exit and back to the hotel.

The remains of the storm clouds scudded across the sky, promising a clear day tomorrow. Or later this morning, Titus amended. The beach was now empty of people, the device that had rescued so many disassembled and removed. The locals must have gone back to their homes, and the sailors to one of the hotels or boarding houses.

The three masts of the schooner were now clearly visible tilted toward the water's surface, as was the part of the hull grounded by the sandbar offshore. As he came to a point directly opposite the shipwrecked vessel, Titus stopped and faced the sea. His clothes had almost dried out during his vigil at the lighthouse, and the wind off the ocean was warm in early July. He shivered even so as the remains of the rain and sea evaporated.

He breathed the air, still heavy with the remnants of the storm, deep into his lungs. If he closed his eyes, he could imagine pirate vessels plying the waters leading into Boston Harbor, waiting for the unwary merchantman. Between the sandbar offshore and the rocks at the end of the peninsula, it was no wonder so many ships fell victim to this coast. He now understood not just in his brain, but in his gut, why this spit of land was called Shipwreck Point.

The tide was coming in, and he had to step back to keep the surf from splashing over his shoes. A useless effort, since they'd already been ruined earlier in the evening. But he wasn't fond of the idea of having wet feet again. When he had to retreat a second time, he knew it was time to head back to his hotel room and snuggle into his warm, dry bed.

As he trod down the beach, his thoughts turned back to the murder and Katie Sullivan. He'd have to talk to her in the daytime. He wasn't sure whether it was to warn her... or protect her. He shook his head. Thoughts like that could get him in a great deal of trouble. Best he keep to himself until it was time for him to return to the city.

CHAPTER 7

TOM HINKLE STOOD in front of Ranson Payne's desk as stiff as a pair of trousers hung on a clothesline during a hard freeze. He'd come to Griffith Hall, the building that housed most of the departments for the town of Whitby, including the office of the chairman of the Board of Selectmen, first thing this morning. Payne thought he was hiding something. Hinkle was making too much of an effort to keep his face emotionless; the furrows on his forehead gave him away.

"Did everything go as planned last night?" Payne asked.

Hinkle cleared his throat as he stuck a finger inside his collar and wedged out some space to breathe. "The schooner wrecked on the sandbar."

Payne felt the pressure build behind his eyes. He hated evasiveness. "That's not what I asked you."

Hinkle swallowed hard. He seemed to have trouble doing it. "Cooper didn't want to put out the light."

Payne's eyebrows raised. The thought of the hold full of fine Kentucky bourbon sliding past Shipwreck Point and making it all the way to Boston put a knot in his stomach. "Why not?"

The henchman looked at his feet. "He didn't say."

"Come now, Hinkle. I've never known Cooper to turn down extra cash. You *did* offer him the cash, right?" Just as the pressure in his head had started to ease, Payne wondered if Hinkle had tried to keep the bribe for himself.

Hinkle's face paled. His mouth opened and closed a few times, resembling nothing so much as a striper when the net is pulled out of the water. Payne feared he'd drop to the floor and start flopping around on the deck.

"Of course I did," Hinkle finally managed to get out. "He wanted the money all right."

"So what was the problem?"

"I don't know. I've never seen him like that, willing to give up the cash rather than take it and douse the oil lamp."

"So the ship wrecked even with the light showing the way?"

Again, Hinkle lowered his eyes. "Not exactly." He dared to peek at Payne for a moment.

Payne met his gaze with one of his own, so filled with steel that it pinned the man's eyes in place. "Hinkle!" Payne roared. "What in blazes happened last night?"

"I had to get a little rough with him. He was in no shape to climb those stairs afterwards, so I put the lamp out myself."

Payne wasn't certain he wanted to know more than that. If he didn't know about it, he wouldn't be forced to deny knowledge of beating the keeper unconscious. Or whatever had happened. Not that Chet Morgan would dare to ask him should he find out about it. He decided to leave things as they were. "Have you told Miller he can head out to the ship?" he asked.

"Not yet. I thought I'd report to you first."

As he should. The pressure in his head eased. His relief at not having to fight a migraine overcame his anger. It was time to let Hinkle off the hook. It appeared as if the job had been accomplished, even if it hadn't gone exactly as planned.

Chapter 8

Katie Sullivan stopped outside the door to Titus Strong's hotel room. She raised her loosely held fist to knock, then held it in the air for a moment as her fist tightened. The newspaper this morning—a special edition of the Whitby Weekly—featured a front-page headline in the largest type she'd ever seen screaming for attention:

Lighthouse Keeper Murdered!

Like any resident of Shipwreck Point, Katie had zeroed in on the story and read every detail. *Who would kill Nate Cooper?* She kept reading the article, hoping for an answer. But the words that began the second paragraph pulsed with danger.

"The murder weapon, a pearl-handled derringer, was left at the scene."

Heart pounding, she'd immediately checked for her gun, opening the drawer to the nightstand where she usually kept it. It wasn't there.

She quickly scanned to the bottom of the story, looking to see if it named the killer. It ended with "The police have no suspect in custody."

They might not have anyone in custody yet, but it wouldn't take long for them to identify the owner of the derringer.

Knowing her only hope of avoiding arrest and being charged with the murder lay with the high-powered lawyer from Boston, she'd hurried to the Seaview Hotel to speak with him. She took a calming breath, then resolutely knocked on the door.

A moment later, Titus Strong opened it. He hadn't put on a tie or jacket yet, and his shirt collar was unbuttoned. His eyes widened as he sucked in a breath. "Mrs. Sullivan. What brings you here this morning?"

"I have to talk to you. Can I come in?" Without waiting for a response, she shouldered her way past him. Other women might faint at the idea of entering a gentleman's room, but it certainly wasn't the first time Katie had done so. In her profession, it was a requirement.

Strong closed the door behind her. A silver tray bearing a coffee service sat on a small table nearby. He gestured at one of the chairs pulled up to it. "Please have a seat. I'd offer you coffee, but since I didn't know you were joining me, I didn't ask for an extra cup."

Coffee was the last thing on her mind. She had a feeling if she drank coffee this morning, her stomach would revolt. It was twisting like a washrag being wrung out after wiping up a spill. "I've already had coffee." She surprised herself by the natural tone of her voice.

"I hope you don't mind if I have some." He sat in the other

chair, the one with a cup and saucer in front of it, and proceeded to pour his coffee, adding sugar and cream before taking a drink.

Katie's foot started tapping of its own volition. There wasn't time for this. At any moment, she was sure Chief Morgan would arrive to arrest her. She took hold of the paper which she'd tucked under her arm before coming here and held it up for Strong to see. "Have you seen this morning's paper?"

Strong calmly took it from her hand and opened it up. "Not yet."

She waited while he read the story. She couldn't help but fidget, adding a rub of her cheeks to the tapping of her foot.

When he was done reading, he folded the paper in half and handed it back to her. "Very interesting. I suppose there aren't many murders in Whitby?"

He was missing the point. "Didn't you see what killed him?"

Strong took another sip of his coffee before nodding his head. "And why is that of interest to you?"

"I think it's my gun. I looked for it this morning, and it wasn't where I usually keep it. When I tried to remember when I'd last seen it, I realized it was during the argument I had with Nate Cooper."

Strong wiped his lips with a napkin and sat up straighter in his chair. "Not afterwards?"

She shook her head. "I must have dropped it that night in all the excitement. I don't remember having it when I got back to the Honey House."

"That's unfortunate." Strong's posture relaxed, and he tented his fingers in front of his lips. His eyes narrowed. He appeared to be thinking very hard. "Did you kill him?"

Katie's jaw dropped. She'd come to Titus Strong because she thought he was the one person in Shipwreck Point who wouldn't think she'd killed Nate Cooper. At least, she'd hoped so. "No."

In a conciliatory tone, he said, "I had to ask. Where were you last night? I didn't see you in the gambling room, and you didn't join the crowd on the beach when the schooner wrecked on the sandbar."

She licked her lips. Staring at her gloved hands folded in her lap, she said, "At the Honey House, of course." She raised her eyes to meet his. "It's my business."

"Can anyone confirm that you were there?"

Her hands started trembling. She was glad they were in her lap and not anywhere Strong could see them. She cleared her throat. "Unfortunately, no. I was in my room working on my accounts."

His mouth quirked up on one side.

"What? Don't you think I have to keep accounts just like any other business?"

"It's not something I would have thought of you doing."

Anger stopped the shaking. She crossed her arms over her chest. "I'm a businesswoman. I manage my business. Why do you think I've been so successful at it?"

He raised his hands as if to ward her off. "Okay, okay. Point taken."

She wondered what he knew that wasn't in the newspaper article. "The paper says you were there last night."

"I was. Officer Kelley and I noticed the light was out at the same time and went out to the lighthouse together."

"Was there any clue pointing to the killer other than my

gun?" She realized she'd admitted the derringer was hers. That was probably a mistake. She hadn't seen the gun herself. She had no way of knowing it was hers. But a sinking feeling in her chest told her it had to be. She couldn't think of any other women who carried a gun, and a derringer definitely wasn't a man's weapon.

Strong must have noticed the slip. "Have you seen the murder weapon?"

"No, but *you* have. You also saw my derringer the night of the argument." The man was annoying her. Perhaps she should consult a different lawyer. The only problem with that was, as far as she knew, there wasn't another criminal attorney in Shipwreck Point.

"Mrs. Sullivan, I have to admit that the derringer looked very much like your gun. Do you have the serial number?"

Confused for a minute, she thought he meant the serial number of the murder weapon. Then she realized he meant her gun. "I did. I know it was written on the bill of sale when I bought it." She wracked her memory for where she might have put that now-important document. She had no idea where it was.

"I think you should locate that bill of sale. With it, we'll be able to prove that the murder weapon doesn't belong to you."

"Or that it does." She felt sick to her stomach.

Titus Strong nodded. "Without it, I'm relatively certain the police will assume the derringer found at the murder scene is yours as soon as someone remembers you own one."

That surprised Katie. She would have thought Strong would have already told the police that he recognized it. "You didn't tell them that?"

"No. I had a feeling I might be doing business with you—my business—and didn't think I should disadvantage my client."

She'd almost laughed when Strong mentioned doing business with her. By the clarification he'd made, he must have noticed. But she focused on the end of his statement. For the first time since she'd seen the newspaper this morning, there was a ray of hope in her life. "You will accept me as a client, then?"

"I will. Now, if you'll go back to the Honey House, I think I need to visit the police station and see what progress Chief Morgan and his officers have made on the investigation."

CHAPTER 9

TITUS SAT QUIETLY for a few minutes after Katie Sullivan left. Her face looked older in daylight than it had a few nights ago. The crow's feet around her eyes placed her closer to his mother's age than his. Or maybe the haggardness of her face was because of worry.

It seemed as if, despite his misgivings about the situation, he had himself a new client. Like most clients, she hadn't told him the whole truth. She'd avoided looking at him when she said she was at the Honey House last night. Generally, that was a good sign that a person was lying. He wondered where she had really been.

When enough time had passed for Katie to have left the hotel, Strong got up. He went to the closet and started to reach for a tie. He stopped before his hand touched it. This wasn't Boston. This was Whitby, a summer town that catered to sun and surf and people on vacation. Putting on a tie and jacket would signal that his visit to the police station was an official one. Although he'd told Katie he'd represent her, he didn't want to tip his hand to Chief Morgan.

As he descended the staircase to the lobby, he realized he didn't know where the police station was. He stopped at the reception desk to ask.

"Ah, that's easy, sir," said the clerk, a young man who looked about the right age to be working summers at the hotel to pay for college. "It's on Spyglass Hill."

That told Strong no more than he already knew. The clerk must have noted his perplexity, because he hurried to add, "On the same side of the Point as the ferry dock. It's a ways south, though. You might want to take a cab. Shall I get one for you?"

"That's not necessary," Strong said. "I'd prefer to walk."

"As you wish. Take Steamboat Avenue off Mayfield, then. You know where that is?"

"Of course. I walked over to the ferry dock down Steamboat Avenue yesterday."

"Good, good." The clerk nodded his approval. "Keep your eye out for Spyglass Lane and follow that to the end. Turn onto Griffith Road. The police station will be on your left."

The directions sounded simple enough. Strong took a moment to go over them in his mind, a way of fixing them there so he wouldn't get lost.

"Is there anything else I can do for you today?"

"No, thank you."

By the time he reached Spyglass Hill, he regretted not taking the clerk's offer of a cab. The way Spyglass Lane curved up an incline as he approached the town center confirmed that he was headed toward the right place. But now that the sun had risen higher in the sky, his shirt was damp with sweat a short distance into his trip.

He stopped at the end of the road to take in the view. Boston Harbor stretched out below him, the harbor islands dots of bright green in a sea of dark olive. Puffy clouds floated by overhead in an otherwise clear sky. An egg-shaped green, or common, took up the center of the hill. A typical New England white wooden church was at the far end of the green, the only building on it. Griffith Road separated the green from the municipal buildings on the other side.

There was some kind of monument built on the common close to the water. Curious, Strong strode off across the grass to see what it was. When he reached it, he discovered a memorial to the heroes of Whitby who had lost their lives in the Revolutionary War, a piece of polished granite carved with their names. Above the names, the Betsy Ross flag with its thirteen stripes and thirteen stars in a circle had been sculpted into the stone.

He was procrastinating and he knew it. He told himself the sooner he went to the police station, the sooner he'd be able to return to his hotel and his vacation. With any luck, the police had already arrested the person who had killed Nate Cooper.

Strong headed back the way he'd come. A sign for the Whitby Police Department hung over the door of a building close to the intersection of Griffith Road with Spyglass Lane. A schoolhouse had been built on one side of the police department and the fire department was on the other. He opened the door to his destination, hoping Tim Kelley would be in and not out on some police business.

Officer Kelley stood at a counter opposite the entrance. He

was studying something on the countertop, but he looked up at the sound of the door opening.

"Good day, Mr. Strong. What can I do for you?"

"Good day, Officer Kelley. I'm glad I found you in. I was wondering what progress has been made in the murder investigation."

"Nothing much, yet. I spent the morning questioning people who might have seen Nate Cooper earlier in the evening, but couldn't find any who had. He stopped at Jake's for a fried clam plate in the afternoon. The waiter remembers him saying something about needing to get ready for the storm coming in, so he assumed Cooper had returned to the lighthouse shortly after to take care of that."

Not wanting to open up a can of worms, but knowing it would be strange for him not to mention it, Strong asked, "Anything on the derringer?"

Tim Kelley glanced toward the door behind him that led to the back area of the police station. He lowered his voice and said, "We both know whose derringer it is. You saw it the other night when Katie Sullivan aimed it at Nate Cooper, same as me. Eventually, Chief Morgan will figure it out, if he hasn't already."

"Is there some reason you're not telling him?"

"I think there has to be another explanation as to why Mrs. Sullivan's gun was found at the crime scene. I'm hoping I'll find out what that is after questioning enough people. The problem is, I don't know who to ask. I've been to all his usual haunts, and no one saw him after he was at Jake's."

"How much longer do you think we have before Chief Morgan remembers the derringer?" What he was really asking was how intelligent Morgan was and how driven he was to solve this murder.

Tim Kelley understood the question. "Morgan might be lazy and arrogant, but he's not stupid. I'm surprised he hasn't remembered what we saw already."

Kelley flinched as the door to the back offices opened. When Titus Strong saw it was the person they'd just been discussing, he knew why.

"What are you doing here, Kelley? You're supposed to be out finding witnesses."

"I have, sir. Since it was so close to lunchtime, I came back to fill out a report of what I've found so far before I went to get something to eat."

"And what have you found out?"

Kelley shook his head. "Not much, chief. Nate Cooper didn't spend a whole lot of time in town yesterday, and I haven't found anyone who will admit to being at the Point yet."

Morgan finally noticed Titus standing there observing this interchange. "What are you doing here?"

Taking his cue from what Tim Kelley had said, he replied, "I was taking a stroll around town this morning. Since it's my first visit to Whitby, I wanted to see the sights. When I spotted the police station, I thought I'd stop in and find out if Officer Kelley would like to join me for lunch."

"We were discussing where we might go, and I told him about the pub." Strong was impressed with how quickly Officer Kelley embellished his lie. The policeman was turning out to be a valuable ally in a town where Titus knew very few people.

CHAPTER 10

TIM KELLEY TOOK a deep breath and let it out slowly after they left the police station. "That was tense."

"I imagine so," Strong said. "I wonder if having lunch together isn't a mistake. I don't think Chief Morgan likes me very much."

"I'm sure he doesn't." Kelley grinned as they strode down Griffith Road past the fire station. "You're everything he never will be: intelligent, wealthy, cultured, with a social status he can only dream of."

Strong couldn't disagree with that without betraying more of his personal history than he cared to, but rather than focus on all his good qualities—he had plenty of bad ones, as well—he asked about something that had been bothering him ever since he'd gotten to the top of Spyglass Hill. "I'm surprised you built the police and fire departments up here. Travel on Spyglass Lane has to be pretty slow if there's a fire burning down on

Mayfield Road."

Kelley looked surprised, then pointed toward the road between the police station and the fire station. "That's Center Street. It goes straight down to Mayfield. Only tourists take Spyglass Lane. It's more picturesque."

Strong snorted a laugh. "I suppose that's why the desk clerk at the Seaview Hotel told me to go that way."

"I'm sure it was."

They were almost even with the church by now, and Tim Kelley took a left onto a street leading away from the common. A block later, he led the way into the Lookout Pub. The smell of tobacco smoke and stale beer greeted them as Kelley opened the door. He led the way to a booth and slid in on one side. Titus sat opposite.

A waiter, who wore a vest over his white shirt but no jacket, appeared at tableside before Titus had a chance to look at the bill of fare printed on a card lying at the center of the table. "What may I serve you gentlemen?"

"Will you trust me to order?" Kelley asked.

Since the policeman must eat here often, Titus thought that was probably his best option. He nodded.

"Two corned beef specials and two mugs of Boston beer."

"Make mine root beer," Titus amended.

"I'll have that out for you in a minute."

Kelley lit up a cigarette and let the smoke out with a sigh. "The chief doesn't like smoking on duty," he explained, then stopped and looked closely at Titus. "You don't mind, do you? I'll put it out if it's a problem."

"Enjoy your cigarette, Officer Kelley."

"Here, here, I'll have none of that 'Officer Kelley' business.

As long as the chief isn't within earshot, you can call me Tim."

"And I'm Titus," the lawyer said with a smile as he held out his hand. Tim didn't hesitate a second. He shook it with a firm grip. Titus felt the tension ease out of his body. Exchanging first names and a handshake showed him he and Tim understood one another.

At that point, the waiter arrived with two mugs, and they each picked one up and took a long swallow. After wiping the foam from his lips, Titus asked, "How long have you been a policeman?"

"Eight years," Tim said proudly. "Six years on the Boston Police, two in Whitby—or Shipwreck Point, as most people call it."

"That's a considerable amount of time." Thinking back to their talk about Joe Kelley, Titus said, "I'm surprised you didn't follow your grandfather into the family business."

"My grandfather is still trying to convince me to become a fisherman, but I think being a policeman is less dangerous." He sighed as his eyes took on a vacant stare directed somewhere over Titus's shoulder.

"You sound like you have personal experience with that danger."

The young man's hand shook as he raised his cigarette to his lips and drew in more smoke. Twin clouds streamed from his nostrils as he let it out. His gaze became focused as he returned it to the face of the lawyer. "That I do. My dad followed in his father's footsteps. He was out with a boat late in the season, and a storm overtook them. He washed overboard while trying to pull in a net."

"I'm sorry to hear that." Titus regretted the turn the

conversation had taken, but he couldn't have known about Tim Kelley's father.

The waiter brought two huge plates of corned beef piled high on dark rye bread and set them down in front of the diners. "Did you need anything else?"

"Not for me," Titus said. He took a taste of his sandwich and was surprised by how good it was. "I was encouraged to hear that you don't think Katie Sullivan is guilty of Nate Cooper's murder. Does the chief share your point of view?"

Tim chewed and swallowed, then shook his head. "Like I said, as soon as he remembers who owns the derringer we found, he'll probably have me arrest her."

"I met Mrs. Sullivan in the gambling room of the Seaview Hotel my first night in town, but I don't know her very well." He carefully omitted their walk on the boardwalk. "What about her makes you think she's not guilty?"

"I've known Mrs. Sullivan since I was a little boy. There weren't so many people living on Shipwreck Point back then. Only the Whitby Hotel had been built, and a few widows had turned their homes into guest houses for visitors. You got to know everyone, especially in winter when the tourists had gone home, not to return until the next year."

Tim's history confirmed what Titus has suspected about her age. Mrs. Sullivan must be as skilled with paint and powder as an actress to make herself look so young. "I'm surprised your parents would let a little boy like you associate with her."

Tim's face turned red as he avoided meeting Titus's eyes. "She's not a bad sort. I hear she only took up her current profession after her husband left her. The poor woman doesn't have any other skills, so she makes do with what she has."

"From the quality of her clothes, I'd say she does very well," Titus said.

"Well enough." Tim put his fork down and leaned back. He patted his stomach with a satisfied look. "They make good food here."

"Yes, they do." Strong picked up on the fact that Tim Kelley didn't want to talk any more about Katie Sullivan. That was fine with him. The only reason her occupation concerned him was that it might matter to a jury of her peers, should the case come to trial. But a jury was only made up of men, and Strong assumed they'd be more forgiving of her profession than a woman would be. "Do you eat here often?"

Tim grinned. "Almost every day. I'm not married, and the last time I tried to cook myself a meal, I almost died from it."

Titus smiled back at him, then frowned as he remembered there was one more thing he wanted to ask Tim Kelley about. He slid his hand in his pocket, pulled out the piece of eight, and laid it on the table.

Tim's eyes widened. "Where did you get that?" he whispered.

"I found it on the floor near Nate Cooper's body." Taking his cue from Tim Kelley, Titus also whispered. "It made me think there might be something to the story I heard about there being pirate treasure on a ship sunk off the coast of Shipwreck Point."

"I wouldn't be showing that around. There might be a treasure lying about on the ocean floor nearby... or there might not. Every once in a while, something like that washes up on the beach, especially out on the Point. I wouldn't put much stock in the pirate treasure tale."

"Why not?" Strong asked. "If there is a treasure and Nate Cooper found it, and someone discovered that he found it, isn't it possible that someone is the real killer?"

"Possible, but I'd say that's pretty far-fetched. If old Cooper had found a treasure, he'd most likely be bragging about it, especially after he'd had a few, if you get my drift." Tim looked thoughtful for a minute. "I wouldn't show that to anyone else if I were you."

"Don't you want it as evidence?"

"I don't. The last time some Spanish coins showed up in town, mobs of people came down from Boston looking for more. They overloaded the ferry, and you couldn't get a seat on the train for a week. Dozens hired fishing boats and jabbed at the sand under the water with long pikes. Some of them dove in and swam to the bottom to see what they could find. It was chaos for a while until the get-rich-quick types gave up." He locked eyes with Strong, and said, "You can see why no one who lives in Shipwreck Point wants anything to stir that up again. Having a piece of eight at the murder scene would be the worst thing that could happen. No, I'd prefer you keep it and never show it to anyone else."

The police officer's passionate speech impressed Titus. There must be more to that pirate treasure story than the young man was letting on. He'd have to discretely see if he could find out more about it. But for now, he picked up the bit of silver and hid it in his pocket.

Titus insisted on picking up the check for their lunch. While they waited for two men ahead of them to pay their bill, Titus perused the notices pinned to a board nearby. Most of them were for various services: a blacksmith, a plumber, a tailor. Two cards advertised rooms to let, probably from the boarding houses Tim had mentioned.

"I wonder what's taking so long?" It was a rhetorical question, since Tim wouldn't know any more than he did. He noticed a brightly colored poster behind the cash register and rose up on his toes to read it.

Large red letters on a yellow background announced a "Fourth of July Fireworks Spectacular!" Splashes of colors representing the promised pyrotechnics filled the center of the poster, with the bottom displaying the place and time. Of course, tomorrow was the Fourth of July. It was something Titus hadn't much thought about. He had too many other problems on his mind. But since they were going to shoot off the fireworks from a barge anchored not too far from the Seaview Hotel, Titus thought he would watch them.

His gaze dipped from the poster to check on the progress of the men ahead of them. An envelope was changing hands between the customer and the man behind the cash register. That seemed odd to Titus, so he paid more attention to the transaction. The customer took the envelope, opened it, and peered inside. He widened the opening, then riffled through the contents as if it were a deck of cards. As the last piece fell into place, it looked like nothing so much as a five-dollar treasury note. Judging by the size of the stack, there were a lot more of them in that envelope.

When the "customer" looked up at the cashier, Titus recognized Hinkle, the man who'd been at the poker table with him a few nights ago and later on upstairs at the hotel. Whitby really was a small town.

Hinkle said, "This better not be short."

"It's all there." The cashier's voice trembled slightly.

"I'll be back if it's not." Hinkle's voice carried a threat.

Titus didn't like the tenor of the exchange. Not for the first time, he had to restrain himself from reacting. Hinkle's eyes met his when the man turned to leave. They widened slightly in recognition.

"Good afternoon," Titus said.

Hinkle didn't respond. He shifted his gaze to the door and pushed his companion ahead of him out into the street.

Titus paid for the meal, then, as they exited the pub, said, "I'll walk you back to the police station."

"Wouldn't you rather take the short way down Center Street?" Tim gestured toward the street they were on.

Titus started walking in the opposite direction, forcing Tim to follow him to hear his answer. "No. I'm in no hurry." He lowered his voice. "Did I read that transaction correctly? Was the pub owner handing Mr. Hinkle an envelope filled with money?"

Tim startled, then looked left, right, and over his shoulder before responding. "You saw things right. Hinkle is one of Payne's bagmen."

"And for what reason would a pub owner need to pay off Ranson Payne?"

Tim confirmed what he'd heard from Katie Sullivan.

"Payne controls the liquor licenses in Shipwreck Point. If you want one, you pay him to get it and you pay him to keep it. A pub owner wouldn't have much of a pub if he couldn't serve beer, now would he?"

"No, he wouldn't." And since beer—and other spirits—were one of the major attractions for the town of Whitby, the rest of eastern Massachusetts being dry, there were plenty of other establishments that would absorb the customers from a pub that didn't have them. They were almost to the police station, so Titus hurried to add. "Does Payne control everything in this town?"

Tim pursed his lips. "Pretty much. Listen, I wouldn't make too much of it if I were you. You don't want to get on the wrong side of Ranson Payne. Enjoy your vacation, and when it's over and you go back to Boston, you forget all about the rest of it."

Strong decided not to argue with him. Tim was probably right. It would be different if he were a resident of Shipwreck Point, but he wasn't.

They'd reached the police station by now. "Let me know if anything develops in the homicide investigation."

"I will," Tim said. "Be careful, Mr. Strong. You don't know who you're dealing with."

CHAPTER 11

As long as he was out, Titus decided he'd take the opportunity to update Katie Sullivan on what progress had been made in the murder investigation. She hadn't come to the Seaview Hotel—at least, not while he'd been in the public areas—since he'd told her to go to the Honey House. He'd asked Tim Kelley where it was over lunch. With a sly smile, Tim had given him directions.

Thirty minutes later, he arrived in front of the two-story house located slightly north of, and conveniently equidistant from, the Seaview and Bay Royale Hotels. A porch extended the length of the house and wrapped around one side. Scattered along it were an assortment of wicker chairs and tables, most of them empty this afternoon.

One girl sat in a chair beside the door. She fanned herself in an attempt to counter the summer heat. She'd languidly draped her body in the chair, almost lying rather than sitting in it.

Strong's footsteps echoed on the wooden floor. The girl smiled at him.

"Are you here to see anyone in particular?"

Raising his eyes to answer her, he recognized Emily, the girl whom Nate Cooper had attempted to rape at the hotel. "Emily, isn't it?"

She nodded.

"You look like you've recovered from the incident the other night."

"You saw it?"

He nodded while she peered at him. "Oh, you're the one who told old Nate to let me go."

"That's right."

"I owe you for that." She looked up at him from under long lashes. "Would you like to collect now?"

Strong's throat tightened, and he almost choked as blood rushed to his face. When he had his voice under control, he said, "You don't owe me. I only did what any respectable man would do."

Her face clouded over, and he realized he had insulted her. "Perhaps we'll meet again at a different time," he said, knowing full well he'd never take advantage of her offer of "payment." "Actually, I came to see Mrs. Sullivan. Would she happen to be in?"

"I'm younger," Emily said.

That was obvious to any man with two eyes. Or even one. Or a blind man who listened to her voice. Emily was barely out of her teens. He smiled at the girl. "Indeed you are. But I have some business to discuss with Mrs. Sullivan."

Emily straightened up. "I'll go get her then. You can wait in the parlor." After she stood and turned toward the door, she glanced coyly over her shoulder and asked, "Are you sure you wouldn't like me instead?"

Strong shook his head. He made sure to keep a suitable distance between the two of them as he followed her inside.

Emily waved to the left as they passed an archway off the hall. "In there."

Strong watched her for a moment as she climbed up the staircase in the center of the vestibule, her un-bustled derriere swaying suggestively from side to side. He had no intention of touching her, but certainly he could look.

When Emily had gone out of sight, Titus went into the parlor. Deep red velvet drapes struck a sharp contrast to the gold wallpaper. A carpet with a design in both colors lay on the floor. Matching ivory and gold fabric covered a sofa with an elaborately carved walnut frame, and two chairs created a group. Titus sat on one of the chairs.

A few minutes later, Katie Sullivan entered the parlor. Titus rose to his feet. She wore a floor-length, emerald green dressing gown. "Good afternoon, Mr. Strong. I wasn't expecting anyone to call."

Deep lines around her eyes and mouth and her pale complexion told Titus she hadn't been sleeping.

"I apologize if I've arrived at an inconvenient time. I could come back later, perhaps tomorrow, if you'd prefer."

"No, no." The way her words rushed out bothered him. There was a note of desperation in them. "Please sit down," she said. She sat on the other chair and put her hands in her lap, not folded as much as clenching one another.

He'd better reassure her about her situation. "I thought

you'd like to know what's going on with the investigation into the murder of Nate Cooper."

She bit her lower lip as she nodded.

"At this point in time, you don't have to worry about being arrested." Mrs. Sullivan visibly sagged at his words. He hated to bring back her worry, but she had to know the truth. "At this point in time," he repeated. "Tim Kelley tells me Chief Morgan hasn't remembered that you had a derringer matching the murder weapon. Yet. No one knows if or when that will change, but we have to work on the assumption that eventually it will."

"I'm resigned to that. But I didn't kill him." Her eyes were pleading with him to believe her.

"I don't think you did. But we have to be able to prove it." He took a deep breath. "Is there anyone who can attest to the fact you were here that night?"

He'd asked that question before, but sometimes if you asked the same question in a slightly different way, you got a different answer.

Her eyes glistened with unshed tears as she shook her head. "No." He watched as she got control of herself. The tears receded. She sat up straighter, and her expression became firm and determined. "I was in my room all night. That's why no one saw me. In fact, I've been in my room ever since you told me to stay at the Honey House.

"I'm tired of being cooped up. I'm used to coming and going as I please. I spend my nights at the hotels, looking for clients, which means I talk to a lot of people. I shop, I walk on the beach when I get a chance, I visit my friends. I think I'm going to lose my mind if I have to stay here one more day."

She breathed heavily. Her tirade had returned the color to her face.

Before Titus realized what he was doing, the words popped out of his mouth. "Would you like to go to the fireworks with me tomorrow night?"

What was he thinking? Or had it been he wasn't thinking? She'd sounded so lonely, he couldn't resist trying to ease her pain.

She blinked rapidly, then her eyes widened as she smiled at him. "Would that include popcorn and a walk through the arcade?"

"I didn't know there was an arcade. Or a place where you could get popcorn. You can show them to me tomorrow night. Say, about eight o'clock?"

"I'd be happy to show you. I'll meet you at the bar in Golden Chances."

Titus was about to object. He thought he should pick her up and escort her from the Honey House. Then he realized this wasn't a date. There was no romantic attachment between the two of them. And, as an independent woman, Katie preferred doing things on her own. That was what she was missing, not merely getting out of her room. "I'll see you then."

CHAPTER 12

Katie stood by the bar, sipping a Jack Rose, a cocktail made from applejack and grenadine named after the famous gangster, as she waited for Titus Strong. Her ankles prickled with the stares of many of the men in the room. She'd chosen to wear her lazy daisy, the short skirt she owned for riding her bicycle around Shipwreck Point, and sometimes even into the neighboring town. Scandalous in Boston, it was common attire during the summer on the Point, especially for walking along the beach. She ignored the stares and pointing fingers.

Still, she was relieved when Strong walked through the door. The brass buttons on his navy blue blazer glinted in the light of the chandeliers.

"Good evening, Mrs. Sullivan." Strong scanned her outfit, lingering a moment on her ankles, then quickly returned his gaze to her face.

For some reason, his stare didn't bother her as much as the

others'. She put her glass on the bar. "Good evening, Mr. Strong. Would you like something to drink before we go?"

"I don't think so." He held out his arm to her. She took it.

"It's easiest to walk down Ocean Avenue." Katie steered him through the hotel lobby rather than out to the beach.

"Which way?" Strong asked as they passed through the front door.

"South. It's near the carousel."

Strong raised an eyebrow. "I didn't know there was a carousel either."

Katie laughed. "That's because you're not staying at the Whitby Hotel. Families stay there, and the children love to ride on the carousel, munch on popcorn, and go to the Penny Arcade after a day of swimming."

Her heart felt lighter than it had in days. As they drew closer to it, she could hear the strains of the calliope at the center of the carousel. The carnival sound of it always made her remember her childhood, happy days in summertime when her parents would let her ride as a special treat.

Strong stopped where Ocean Avenue veered to the right, up toward Mayfield Road. The carousel was on their left. A stand in front of it spread the smell of popcorn and roasting peanuts through the nearby surroundings. On the right side of the road, a storefront with a sign reading Penny Arcade occupied a lot a few steps away.

"Would you like to go to the arcade right away, or would you like some popcorn first, Mrs. Sullivan?"

"I don't think we need to be so formal tonight. We're two people out to enjoy themselves. Why don't you call me Katie?"

She could see the doubt in Strong's face. It bothered her.

She'd hoped they could become friends. Then the doubt disappeared and he said, "I don't see why not, Katie."

She returned his smile and felt a little better. "Why, then, Titus, I think I'd like to visit the arcade first."

The clamor of the music machines playing different tunes, along with the animated conversations and exclamations from those trying their hand at the games, made conversation almost impossible. Katie raised her voice as she pointed to a series of devices along one wall. "Have you ever played bagatelle?"

Titus asked, "What does it do?"

"Pulling the plunger releases a ball into the machine. It bounces off the spikes and bumpers and bells and winds up in one of the holes."

"And?"

"Each hole has a different number of points. The one who scores the most points wins." She headed toward the machines. "Come, I'll show you."

Katie fed a nickel into the slot, which released the plunger. She pulled it back, then let go. The tiny ball shot from the tube and around the top of the machine, ricocheting off the various obstacles, bouncing up, down, and sideways. Eventually, the ball's momentum absorbed by the collisions, it settled in one of the holes. "Ten points! Now you try."

Titus took her place and tentatively pulled back the plunger. Tentative had been a mistake. The ball barely got out of the chute, then lazily made its way down the surface of the game and settled at the bottom, missing every hole it came even close to.

Katie smothered a laugh with her hand. "Try again. Put a little more muscle behind it."

This time, Titus scored five points, and he gave her a weak smile.

"Let me show you again. Pull the plunger back firmly and let it go quickly." She demonstrated the technique as she spoke and scored another ten points. "Do you want to try the last one?"

"Of course," Titus said. This time, his ball bounced jauntily off a series of spikes and bumpers, merrily ringing the bells as it zigzagged down the board. "Ten points!" He pumped his fist in the air in victory. He dug his hand in his pocket and pulled out another nickel.

She smothered a laugh at his enthusiasm. Men were just little boys in a larger size. As he was about to put the nickel in the machine, Katie put her hand on his. "Why don't we try one of the other games first? We can always come back to bagatelle later."

He looked disappointed, but followed her to a trio of peephole viewers near the back wall. "These are fun. The pictures move just like they were real. Put your eye near the opening and I'll turn the crank so you can watch."

Titus bent over the viewer. Katie ran the machine. After a few seconds, Titus raised up and blinked his eyes rapidly for a moment. "That was amazing! The man moved and sneezed like he was standing right in front of me. I wonder how they do it."

Katie shrugged. "I don't know. They tell me Mr. Edison thought of it."

Titus was staring at a sign reading Gentlemen Only over a curtained entrance on the back wall. "What's back there?"

Laughter bubbled up inside her. She was having the best time she'd had in years. "A different sort of moving pictures."

She winked at him. "Would you like to go inside and see one?"

His face reddened. "Not tonight."

"If you would, I won't mind. I hear they're quite stimulating."

He shook his head. "What other games can we play?"

She led him to a stand where a man held a handful of darts as he urged potential customers to play.

"Hit a balloon, win a prize!"

"Shall I?" Titus asked.

"Oh, you must! I'd love to have a chalkware doll," she said with a touch of sarcasm. Almost no one won prizes at the arcade. Even if they did, the prizes were more like toys. Nothing of value was given away. The chalkware doll had an enormous head with oval eyes and a mouth wide with surprise. It was very cute. But the attraction wasn't really to win. No, people kept coming back because it was fun to play.

While Titus concentrated on the darts and balloons, Katie's eyes were drawn to the ripple of the curtain on the back wall. Tom Hinkle and one of his cronies stepped out, having a conversation that Katie couldn't hear because of the din. She shivered when he stared at her. The hairs on the back of her neck raised and tickled her skin. There was something about that look that was very unsettling.

She startled at the sound of a balloon popping, breaking eye contact with Hinkle.

Titus let out a victory shout. "Yes!" Then, he added with concern, "Is something wrong, Katie?"

"I'm not sure." She indicated Hinkle with a tip of her head. "I felt like someone had walked on my grave when Hinkle came through the curtain. He gives me the willies sometimes."

Titus pressed his lips together. "Probably with good reason."

She shook off the feeling, then said with a smile, "Come. Let's get some popcorn before the fireworks start."

CHAPTER 13

Titus managed to crack open the peanut shell with one hand, his other being occupied with holding the warm bag, then popped the nuts in his mouth, and savored the taste.

Katie, who had stayed with her original choice of popcorn, tittered and said, "You have quite a talent."

"Necessity is the mother of invention."

The strains of the carousel's calliope faded as they reached the steps leading up to the boardwalk. Titus stopped cracking nuts to offer his arm to Katie for the climb. He breathed in the smell of the sea, then did it again.

"I imagine Shipwreck Point smells better than Boston," Katie said as they walked down the boardwalk.

"It does, indeed. I think I'll have to spend more time here in the summer."

"I'm glad you qualified that statement. Winters can be harsh, with the storms coming in off the ocean, and the waves crashing over the seawall. People still tell stories of the Saxby Gale, which toppled houses from one end of the Point to the other. Then there was the Great Blizzard of 1888, when the snow was up to your waist."

"We got the blizzard in Boston, too," Titus said.

"But not the ice and the tides. Whitby turned into two islands, with the sea covering it from where the Seaview now stands across to the marina. Icicles hung from everything, and you couldn't go outdoors or you'd be pelted with shards of frozen water."

"I'm surprised they built the Seaview where it is then. Aren't they afraid it will be destroyed in the next storm?"

Katie shrugged her shoulders. "They say it was a hundred-year storm, and we're not likely to have another one like it in our lifetimes." She paused to take a handful of popcorn from her bag. "But they built the town on Spyglass Hill because it wasn't the first time that happened. You can't very well have your police and fire departments under water when you're most likely to need them." She tossed the popcorn in her mouth.

"I was wondering about that. They seem so far away from the heart of Whitby's business establishments." Titus ate a few more peanuts. The boardwalk was crowded with visitors, most of them heading in the same direction as they were. "Where can we see the fireworks?"

Katie smiled. "You can see them from almost anywhere if you look up when you hear them go off. But I think you're meaning where the best view is. They float the barge off the beach in front of the bathhouse, so most people stand somewhere near there."

As they were almost to the bathhouse, Titus began looking

for an open space along the railing that faced the water. People had started to line up already, and he was afraid they might have to stand in the center of the boardwalk itself or down on the sand. Finally, he saw an opening they might squeeze into. He pointed toward it. "How about there?"

"That looks like a good spot," Katie agreed.

The two of them found a place where they could stand next to one another once the people already there moved aside a few inches. Titus crumpled his now-empty bag and stuck it in a pocket before leaning against the railing. Down below, the twinkle of sparklers lit up the night as children waved them in the air. Just beneath him, he could see the rapt expression of one boy as he gazed up at the sputtering sparks from the one he was holding.

Not too much later, a boom from the barge announced the beginning of the show as a rocket soared into the air. Accompanied by a chorus of oohs and aahs, its trail lit up the night sky until it reached its apex, when a second, louder boom ended its flight. It was quickly followed by several more, the concussion echoing off the bathhouse behind them. For fifteen minutes or so, exploding colors filled the sky. After a rapid succession of three rockets—a red, a white, and a blue—the crowd sighed its disappointment, knowing the show was over.

Titus took Katie's arm to walk her back to the Honey House.

"I do so love fireworks," Katie said as they turned to join the crowd now headed away from the beach.

"I do, too," Titus said, feeling the same joy and wonder at the display as that little boy with the sparkler he'd seen before it started. "It's a shame we only see them one time a year."

As he stepped into the throng, Titus glimpsed a familiar face watching them through the crowd. He halted and looked closer to make sure.

"What is it?" Katie asked as she followed his gaze. "Oh."

He was sure now from Katie's reaction. Hinkle *was* staring at them. Titus had the feeling he'd been watching them all evening, following them. *Why would he do that?* Titus shivered despite the warm, humid summer air of the beach. He didn't like the way he kept running into Tom Hinkle.

CHAPTER 14

WITH NOTHING ON his agenda until later this afternoon, Strong thought a visit to the lighthouse by daylight was in order. When he inquired at the desk, the concierge told him a trolley ran out to the Point every hour during the summer to allow visitors to see one of Whitby's favorite attractions.

He had just enough time to catch it when it stopped in front of the hotel, so he thanked the concierge and hurried out the Mayfield Road entrance. The clip-clop of horses' hooves announced the trolley's arrival moments before it came into view. It was already half-filled with families, with many of the children carrying brightly colored balloons.

Strong took a seat near the front rather than battle his way through the bobbing balloon forest that had sprouted up in the aisle. Almost everyone stayed on until they reached the end of the road, a loop that circled in front of the near side of the lighthouse. Titus was off the trolley before most of the families had gotten well enough organized to descend the steps together.

He was dismayed to see a police officer he didn't recognize standing in front of the keeper's cottage. At least that partially answered his question as to how many officers were on the Whitby Police force. A minimum of two. He'd been hoping to have another look inside, but something told him keeping people out was the exact reason the officer had been stationed there. He'd have to make the best of the situation he could.

"Good morning, officer."

The man was several years younger than Tim Kelley, barely out of school, and he didn't look too sure of himself. But his voice was strong and steady when he replied. "Good morning, sir. What can I help you with?"

Titus played the curious tourist. "Is this where that man was murdered?"

"It is indeed, sir." He puffed up a bit. "That's why I'm here. I'm protecting the crime scene."

"You don't suppose I could have a look at it?" Although he anticipated the answer, it didn't hurt to try.

The policeman shook his head. "No, no, no, sir." He lowered his voice to a conspiratorial whisper. "Now, if it were just you, I might be persuaded to let you have a look inside for some minor consideration, if you get my drift."

Another confirmation that corruption had penetrated the police department, even though he could have assumed that given Chief Morgan's behavior.

"But if they see you go in"—the policeman looked toward where the crowd of people had spread out over the grounds —"everyone will want to do it."

"I understand perfectly." Then he had a thought. "Who's minding the lighthouse at night now that the keeper is dead? They're not letting it go dark, are they? Not after that boat wrecked and all."

"Ship, sir," the policeman gently corrected him. "Small craft are called boats. Large ones are ships."

"The ship, then," Titus said agreeably.

"Temporarily, Mr. Allen Payne, Mr. Payne's nephew. I imagine he'll get the job permanent, if his wife consents to living so far from town."

"And if she doesn't?" Strong asked.

The policeman shrugged. "That will be up to the Board of Selectman. They'll probably hold a special meeting to decide."

"I see."

"Hey, there," the policeman called out, looking to the left of where they stood. "Get down before you break your neck." A boy roughly eight years old had climbed up the steps to a second door to the keeper's cottage and was swinging from the railing that surrounded the small porch. "Excuse me, sir." Without waiting for an acknowledgment, he trotted down the rocky yard.

Now that he had a chance, Titus tried the door. Locked. He should have expected that. It appeared as if he wasn't going to get a second look at the crime scene today. Rather than ride back on the trolley with the din of a dozen children on holiday, he thought he'd walk back to the Seaview.

As he followed Mayfield Road back toward the central portion of Whitby, Titus noticed that Shipwreck Point bulged in a protrusion of land to the west. Modest homes clustered along the shore, and a series of wooden docks, rougher and more weather-beaten than those in the marina, jutted out into the water. The docks were nearly empty now. Titus guessed this was where the men who made their living selling the fish they caught docked their boats.

A large vessel was moored at the dock farthest from him. Unlike the rest of the area, there was a lot of activity around that boat—*or was it a ship?*—and that made Titus curious. He picked up his pace to see what was going on.

A net dangled from a crane that rose from the deck of the ship aft of the mainmast. A man with a hand truck carrying a barrel pushed past Titus. The words Fine Kentucky Bourbon were stenciled on the side of the barrel.

A crewman lowered the net to the deck and detached it from the crane's hook. He rolled several barrels out of the net toward a waiting group of workers, each man with his own hand truck. When the last man approached, pushing a barrel in front of him, Titus positioned himself so he'd be able to speak to the dock hand.

"Halloo, there," he said when the man drew close enough. The worker slowed his pace a bit. "What have you got there?"

The man gave him a gap-toothed grin. "Can'tcha read? Bourbon!"

"Is it headed for one of the hotels?" Titus asked.

The worker stopped and wiped his brow with a neckerchief. "Eventually." This time his smile was sly.

"What do you mean by 'eventually'?"

"Right now, it's headed over there." The dock hand pointed in the direction he'd been headed before Titus stopped him.

Following the direction of his finger, Titus observed a path that led from the dock to a fenced-in area. A gate guarded the entrance. Over the gate was a sign that read Payne Salvage Company. *Did Ranson Payne have a finger in every pie in Whitby?* Titus suddenly realized where the whiskey had come from, and it wasn't from a supplier in Boston. "Did that come off the ship that wrecked the other night?"

"Now you're gettin' it."

"Doesn't it belong to the owners of the ship? Or whoever contracted with them for transport?"

"Not anymore. It's salvage, like the sign says."

Titus was going to ask another question, but a beefy man stuck his head and shoulders outside the gate and yelled, "McNeil! Stop lallygagging with the tourists and get that barrel in here."

McNeil shrugged apologetically at Strong and resumed pushing his barrel toward the salvage yard. Titus followed him inside with no hesitation. He spied the man who had yelled inside a little shack a few yards away. Titus assumed he was the foreman. While the dock worker headed toward the back of the yard with his cargo, Titus veered off toward the shack.

"Good morning," he said pleasantly when he got there.

"What's your business here?" the foreman said with a scowl.

"I was just curious about where that barrel of fine bourbon was going to."

"That depends on who pays for it, now doesn't it." The foreman's face transformed into one about to share a confidence, one man of the world to another. He leaned in toward Titus as he said, "I suppose you're wondering where you could get a glass to drink?"

"Mr. McNeil said it might be going to one of the hotels. I'm sure they'd be glad to pay for it, as I'd be glad to pay for a glass or two."

"Well, either them or the insurance company. If it's the insurance company, we'll take it to Long Wharf in Boston and someone there will pick it up."

So, either way, Payne stood to make a profit on the cargo of the wrecked ship. He wondered if the light not working the night of the storm had been just a coincidence. Or had it been purposefully arranged?

CHAPTER 15

Titus strode down the gangplank from the ferry onto Long Wharf pier carrying his suitcase. A row of cabs waited to pick up departing passengers, and Titus stepped up to the first available one.

"Where to, sir?" the cabbie asked.

He gave him his address in the Back Bay and mounted the step into the cab. Since it didn't appear Katie was under imminent threat of arrest, he'd thought it was safe to return to Boston and accompany Victoria to the performance at the Grand Opera House. Safer than not going, which would result in another vitriolic lecture from his wife and a scolding from his father-in-law.

"Good to see you home, sir," the butler said as he took Titus's suitcase from him. "I believe Mrs. Strong is in the parlor."

"Thank you, Barkley." As soon as the butler turned his back,

Titus took a deep breath to center himself and strode into the parlor. Victoria occupied a chair by a window, an embroidery hoop in one hand, needle and thread in another. Her thin, angular body wasn't quite disguised under her voluminous skirts and mammoth mutton sleeves. Her elbows were sharp corners, her torso squeezed small and stiff by her corset. She looked up at the sound of his footsteps.

"So you decided to come home," she said, acid dripping from her words.

"Just for the weekend, Victoria." He bent over and gave her a perfunctory kiss on the cheek.

"How long is it going to take you to 'recuperate'? Father has been asking when you'll return to the office." She jabbed the needle into the cloth in the hoop, fed it up from below, then stared at him as she waited for his answer.

"It will take as long as it takes. I'll speak with him this afternoon." Then, not being able to resist a jab of his own, he added, "I imagine he misses the fees I earn more than he misses me." He was sure the same could be said of Victoria.

"Did you remember our engagements for tomorrow night, then?"

"I did. What else have you planned for us in addition to the performance at the Grand Opera House?" He was sure there were other arrangements. With Victoria, there were always multiple events scheduled around whatever primary activity was taking place.

"We'll be having cocktails before at the Appletons. Afterwards, the Gardners are hosting a dinner. Carrie Gardner is getting engaged to some diplomat's son, and I think they're planning on announcing the engagement then."

Surprised, Titus responded, "I didn't think Carrie was old enough to be engaged."

"You should pay closer attention. She's already nineteen."

"As old as that? I suppose you'll want me to go to the wedding."

"Of course. But you needn't worry. I don't think it will happen for at least a year."

Titus could feel the unspoken undercurrent in the conversation. Victoria had never gotten pregnant, and so they had no children to get engaged or married. He knew she blamed him for the lack, but as far as he knew, everything with him was functioning perfectly. But a physician had assured her it couldn't possibly be her fault, and so it must be Titus's.

"I think I'll go upstairs and unpack. I also want to make sure my tailcoat and trousers are clean and pressed for tomorrow night."

Victoria resumed her stitching, and Titus made his escape. Speaking with Victoria was always exhausting. Socializing with her was more so.

Ten years ago, he'd thought he was in love with her. Graduating at the top of his class from Harvard, he'd been bowled over by the opportunity to work with Gideon Thornton in the prestigious Boston law firm. He'd never imagined such things possible in his impoverished childhood, but he'd proved they were. He'd learned to speak and dress the part of a successful lawyer. When invited to have dinner at the senior partner's home, he'd fallen in love with the lifestyle the partner lived. When Victoria had shown interest in him, he'd fallen in love with her.

But from his current vantage point, that period of his life

had all been an illusion. The plain people of Shipwreck Point were more to his taste. But his career would be ruined if it were touched by the scandal of divorce. No, better to continue the charade than to think about leaving his wife permanently.

And now, he supposed, he should wash up and change and go to the law firm's offices to speak with his father-in-law, who was also his boss. It wasn't something he was looking forward to.

By late Sunday afternoon, Titus was leaning on the railing of the ferry, the wind off the water blowing away the stench of the city, making him feel clean again. He breathed deeply, sucking in the salt air, easing the tightness that had gripped him for the past three days.

He'd spent an uncomfortable hour with Gideon Thornton on Friday. No matter how many times Titus tried to explain his discomfort with helping a murderer avoid conviction, the response had been that of a headmaster admonishing a wayward schoolboy.

His place was not to determine guilt or innocence. That was what the judge and jury were for. His job was to defend his client to the best of his ability, pay no attention to the evidence condemning the miscreant's lies (although the senior partner hadn't put it in those words), work hard to refute that evidence, or at least cast enough doubt on its veracity to make the jury come back with a not-guilty verdict.

His conscience had a problem with that.

Then there had been his wife and her society friends. His face had grown stiff from the smile he wore for hours on end, turned his skin into a mask until he hardly felt human. At least

Victoria had announced that she was going to Newport to visit friends—with or without him—for the rest of the summer. There would be no more functions to attend until fall.

The ferry neared the dock, and Titus was eager to go ashore. Finally, it pulled into the slip, the lines fore and aft made secure, and the gangplank lowered to allow the passengers to debark.

This time, he didn't mind the throngs of noisy children herded by their parents as they reached dry land again. He smiled at the pickpockets and the confidence men urging the new arrivals to play their games of chance, which really weren't games of chance at all. All the activity reminded him of a carnival, so much so that he heard the hurdy-gurdy music of a carnival in his head.

Rather than take a cab back to the Seaview Hotel, Titus walked along the dock, hoping to find the Arvilla with the thought of going fishing tomorrow. He'd missed talking to Joe Kelley, and catching a few stripers sounded like the cure for his city malaise.

He was pleased to find the sloop tied up, looking as if it had just returned from a charter trip. Four men with sunburned hands and faces were getting off the boat, creels full of fish in their hands and satisfied smiles turning their cheeks into bright red apples.

Titus waited while they cleared the sloop, watching Joe Kelley make the boat tidy now that his passengers were out of the way. He waved at the old fisherman, trying to get his attention. Which he did.

Kelley stopped what he was doing and scrambled over the side of the sloop onto the dock. When he got close enough that Titus could smell the fish on him, Kelley pushed his face forward and yelled, "Where the hell have you been, man? Katie's been arrested."

CHAPTER 16

Titus's stomach felt like someone had reached inside it and turned on the spigot to a tank full of acid. "When did that happen?"

Getting Titus's attention had calmed Joe Kelley down. In a more reasonable voice, he said, "Late Friday afternoon. She'd just arrived at the Seaview and taken her place at the bar when Chief Morgan showed up with a warrant for her arrest."

Titus pressed his lips together. A muscle near his jawbone twitched in response. "I should have let you know where I was staying in Boston."

"Boston, was it? No wonder no one saw you all weekend."

"I had something to take care of." Titus had no desire to elaborate on why he'd gone to the city. "I didn't think they had enough evidence to charge her with the crime."

Kelley smirked. "Have you not learned enough about Shipwreck Point yet to realize evidence isn't always required here?"

"I'm starting to get the picture. Has her bail been set?"

"Bail? Do you think they'll be letting her out, then?"

"It's customary to at least have a hearing. Speaking of which, where is the courthouse?" While he knew where everything was in Boston, it dawned on him that Whitby was in a totally different county. Usually the courthouse and the office of the district attorney were located in the largest city in a county or in one centrally located. He was a little fuzzy as to what that might be here.

"Up on Spyglass Hill. Surely you noticed it when you went to lunch with Timmy? It's on the corner where you turn to go to the pub."

"In Whitby?" Titus asked in amazement, even as he noted that Tim had told his grandfather about the lunch.

"Do you think Ranson Payne would let some other town control the court?"

"Does he really swing that much clout?"

Kelley cocked an eye toward Strong. "Let's just say he's well-connected."

Titus mulled this for a while. If Payne was as powerful in Whitby as Boss Tweed had been in New York, even if it was on a smaller scale, he'd have to feel his way carefully in this case. "I take it there hasn't been an examination, then?"

The old fisherman shook his head.

"Well, then that's to our advantage. They'll have to do that if they plan to hold her very long. I'd better go see Katie." He paused a moment. "I suppose the jail is also on Spyglass Hill?"

Kelley nodded. "Aye, but you most likely won't be gettin' into it today."

"Why not?"

"It's Sunday, man. Even in Boston, I doubt you'd be able to get access to a jail unless you wanted to have a few at the pub and get arrested for public drunkenness."

"I don't think that would be my best plan of attack." Titus had forgotten the day in his agitation over Katie's arrest. Monday morning seemed a lifetime away.

"Will you find me a cab, please?" Titus Strong said to the doorman of the Seaview Hotel. He lifted his chin and stretched his neck as he tried to find a comfortable position inside his freshly starched collar. Although the town center was within walking distance, he didn't want to arrive sweating and disheveled. He wanted to appear professional for his first official meeting with Chief Morgan. He'd even stopped at the hotel barber for a haircut and a trim of his beard and mustache, something he hadn't bothered with for the night out in Boston.

"Certainly, sir."

A few minutes later, Strong was riding through the streets of Whitby. It didn't take long to reach the police station, and after paying the hack, he went through the front door. Tim Kelley stood behind the counter.

"Good morning, Mr. Strong. What can I do for you today?" His tone was formal, with none of the friendliness they'd shared over lunch the other day.

"I'm here to talk to Katie Sullivan."

Officer Kelley rubbed the back of his neck, realized what he was doing, and dropped his hand to his side. "I'm not sure that will be possible. You'll have to speak with Chief Morgan first."

"Is he in?" Titus Strong wasn't used to being denied what he wanted. It annoyed him that Tim Kelley hadn't just showed him to a place where he and Katie could talk.

"Yes, sir. I'll see if he's available." Kelley disappeared through the door leading to the back of the police station for a few minutes. When he returned, he said, "Chief Morgan will see you. Go through that door and walk all the way to the back. His office is on the left."

When he reached the end of the dingy hallway, Titus knocked on the door, then opened it and walked in without waiting for a response. Two could play at power games.

"Good morning, Mr. Strong. Have a seat." Morgan waved at the chairs in front of his desk. The movement set his double chins to jiggling.

Once Titus was seated, he said, "I'd like to see my client."

The chief's eyebrows twitched, but he had enough self-control to keep from showing his surprise with more than that. "When did Mrs. Sullivan become your client?"

He glared at Morgan with narrowed eyes. "As soon as you arrested her. I assume you had a warrant when you did that?"

The chief folded his hands on his desk and returned the stare. His eyes were shark eyes, showing as little emotion as if he were dead. "We follow the law here in Whitby just like in Boston, Mr. Strong."

"Might I see a copy?"

Morgan held Strong's gaze for a moment longer, then switched his attention to the inbox on the corner of his desk, which held a stack of manila file folders. He lifted the top one and pulled out the next in the pile. He put the folder on the desk in front of him and opened it.

Titus made a slight effort to read—upside down—part of each paper as Morgan went through them, but the folder was too far away for him to have a clear view.

Morgan found the one he was looking for and passed it over to Titus.

The lawyer read the one-page form. The blanks had been filled in with the essential facts: the date, the accused, the crime. The reasons for the accusation weren't there; he hadn't expected them to be. He'd have to get that information from the District Attorney. He passed the paper back to Morgan. "May I see my client now?"

The chief stalled as he put the warrant back in the precise place from which he'd withdrawn it, closed the folder, and put it back in his inbox. "I'll give you a few minutes with her." He stood and came out from behind his desk, his bulk filling the small space.

Titus felt as if a tide of flesh was pushing him out of the office, and it took no urging for him to lead the way into the hall. He stepped back and pressed himself against the wall to allow Morgan to get by him.

The chief ponderously plodded toward the lobby of the police station. Halfway there, he pointed to a door. "You can wait in the interrogation room."

Strong dipped his head in acknowledgment and put his hand on the doorknob. He waited before turning it.

Morgan's words from the outer office were clearly audible. "Tim, get Mrs. Sullivan from her cell and bring her to the interrogation room." His voice lowered, and Titus had to strain his ears to hear the rest of what he said. "Take your time about it. I want our fancy lawyer from Boston to sweat a little."

"Yes, sir," Tim Kelley's voice said loud and clear.

Titus caught sight of Morgan's foot as it appeared in the opening at the end of the hall, so he quickly stepped into the interrogation room, closing the door behind him.

Chapter 17

Titus drummed his fingers on the interrogation room table, then looked at his pocket watch again. It had been almost thirty minutes since Morgan had told him to wait here to speak to Katie. Officer Kelley was obeying his chief's instructions, probably more strictly than he needed to.

Finally, the door opened and Katie Sullivan walked through.

"I'll be back in fifteen minutes to escort Mrs. Sullivan back to her cell," Kelley said.

"Make it thirty," Titus replied.

The police officer hesitated and looked like he was going to object to Strong's order, then nodded and closed the door.

"How far away is the jail?" Titus asked Katie Sullivan.

She looked surprised. "Why, it's just downstairs."

Titus fumed as his nostrils flared. "They've kept me waiting here for half an hour." Then, taking notice of the lines around her eyes and the set of her mouth, he said, "I apologize for the rant. How are you?"

"I've been in worse situations than this. I'll survive." She sat tall and straight, every muscle taut.

Some day he'd have to find out what had been worse than being arrested for murder, but that could wait for another time. "Tell me what happened."

Her posture eased slightly. "From what I hear, Chief Morgan started asking questions about who owned the derringer you found at the lighthouse. It's obviously not a man's weapon. As I feared, he remembered my argument with Nate Cooper at the hotel and went back to question people who witnessed that. I'm surprised he didn't talk to you." She paused and looked at Titus.

The look told him her last statement had really been a question, so he answered it. "I went into Boston for the weekend. I imagine he asked for me at the hotel, and they told him I was away."

"That explains it, then. Anyway, someone remembered my derringer, and when Chief Morgan showed him the gun they'd found, the person recognized it as being the same as the one they'd seen earlier in the week."

"Do you know how it got out to the lighthouse?"

She shrugged her shoulders. "All I know is it was missing when I went to look for it in the drawer of my nightstand the next morning. I must have dropped it sometime during the altercation, perhaps when I went to pull Emily away from Cooper."

He cupped his chin in one hand and stroked his fingers across the stubble that had already started to sprout. *Was she telling the truth about the gun?* Had someone who had seen it the night of her fight with Cooper picked it up? But why would they keep it rather than returning it to its owner? Had the murder of Nate Cooper been premeditated, and the murderer already planning to frame Katie Sullivan for it? Or was Katie lying about losing it, hoping to cast blame on someone else?

"Let's take another tack," Titus said. "Are you *sure* no one saw you at the Honey House on the night of the murder?"

Katie visibly sagged. "I've asked every one of my girls. None of them remembers whether I was there or not. Even if one of them did, I think she might be too frightened of having to testify in court to step forward. Even the hint of getting involved with the legal system scares most of them, since they've all been arrested before."

Strong considered this, wondering if there was a way of encouraging one of the girls to talk. Bribes or threats were the usual inducements, but he'd never put them in his arsenal. "I'll be honest with you. Things are not looking good." He heard her suck in a breath, and her eyes grew shiny. "But the evidence is mostly circumstantial. No one saw you near the lighthouse, either."

"So there's hope?"

"There's always hope." He smiled at her, trying to reassure her, but he saw a lot of work in his future. *So much for his vacation by the sea.* "I'll start forming a team to defend you. I can do most of the investigation myself, but I'll need a girl to type and take notes and such."

"Will it cost very much money?" Katie asked. "I have some saved, but the Honey House makes most of its money during the summer months, and summer has barely started."

"Don't worry about that for now. With any luck, you'll be

out of jail shortly. They'll have to prove probable cause at the preliminary hearing to keep you." That reminded him he hadn't gotten information on the hearing yet. "Do you know when that will be?"

She shook her head. "I didn't know to ask about it."

"I'll see if I can find out from Morgan. Meanwhile, keep your chin up." He tried to smile at her, but he felt his lips form a rictus rather than a genuine grin. He went for irony instead. "I'm the famous Boston lawyer who got a known murderer off last month."

At that minute, Tim Kelley knocked, then opened the door. "Time's up."

Titus rose from his chair, and Katie did the same. She glanced anxiously at the policeman. Trying to reassure her, Titus said, "Don't worry. These things always seem bleaker than they are."

She gave him a weak smile. "Perhaps. I do feel better now that you're working to free me."

"Mrs. Sullivan, I have to take you back now," Tim Kelley insisted.

Katie turned and went with the policeman. Meanwhile, Titus made his way back to Morgan's office.

Morgan hadn't been very helpful when Titus questioned him about the timing of the preliminary hearing, answering his questions with the equivalent of "I'll let you know." He'd have to check in at the courthouse later, see if the clerk had the court date on the docket. Meanwhile, he was happy to see Tim Kelley had returned to the front of the police station.

"Where would a defense attorney find reasonable temporary

office space to rent?"

"You're opening an office?"

"A *temporary* office."

Tim Kelley thought for a minute, then said, "I don't think there's anything available on Spyglass Hill. You might try Griffith Hall, but it won't be inexpensive. Perhaps on one of the streets at the base of the hill." It didn't take him long to add, "Will you be needing a secretary?"

"Is there a reason you're asking?" Strong countered.

"It's just that a girl I went to school with is looking for a job. She knows typing and shorthand and is very reliable."

"I might be able to use her on a temporary basis. *Temporary.* If that's acceptable to her, I'll let you know when I've found a place to set up shop, and you can send her around to see me."

"That would be great, Mr. Strong." Then, as if remembering that he shouldn't be so chummy with the defender of Morgan's primary suspect, he glanced down the hall before adding, "It might be better if you let my grandfather know."

"Did you get in trouble for having lunch with me the other day?" Titus wanted to know what was what.

"Just talk to the old fisherman."

Titus said nothing. Tim Kelley's face said it all, and there was no need to confirm his suspicions. Someone—probably Chief Morgan—had let him know that he shouldn't be getting chummy with a defense attorney, particularly *this* defense attorney.

CHAPTER 18

TAKING TIM KELLEY'S advice, Strong headed east down Central Avenue toward the center of Whitby. As he passed all the homes, he wondered where Tim thought he could rent an office. All he saw was a mix of summer bungalows and year-round houses. You could tell the difference by which ones had chimneys. But nothing that looked like an office building, if you didn't count the doctor's office that was a part of a house on the corner of Revere Street.

He reached Mayfield without locating a likely building and decided to go back to the Seaview and make inquiries there. But he needed to go no farther than a few yards before passing a real estate office in a small two-story building with a sign in the front window saying Offices for Rent. He went inside.

"May I help you, sir," a young man with a neatly trimmed mustache asked eagerly. He had looked up from a desk near the door, one of four laid out in the spacious storefront.

"I saw your sign and was wondering if I might rent an office on a temporary basis."

"How long would you be needing it, sir? Till the end of the summer? Or longer?"

Strong had been afraid he wouldn't be able to get a lease for less than a year, but the young man's response reminded him that Whitby was a summer town. There must be dozens of businesses that were only open in the summer. "I'm not exactly sure. Would it be possible to get a month-to-month lease?"

The young man furrowed his brow. "Let me check with Mr. Murphy. If you'll have a seat, I'll be right back."

Titus settled himself in one of the spare chairs in front of the desk and watched as the young man strode back to an older gentleman at the desk in a rear corner. Gray streaked his hair and beard, and deep lines crinkled around his eyes. If Strong had to guess, his erect posture and confident attitude suggested Mr. Murphy was the owner of the business.

The young man talked animatedly with Mr. Murphy, who didn't seem to be interested in a short-term lease. Then the younger man waved toward Titus, causing Murphy to glance in his direction. The glance turned into a stare, and Murphy got up from his desk and hurried forward.

"Mr. Strong," he said heartily as he stuck out his hand. "Brian Murphy at your service. It's an honor to meet such a famous lawyer."

Titus rose from his chair to shake the man's hand. While he might be a graybeard, Murphy's voice was strong and his eyes sharp and clear. "The honor is mine, sir."

"I hear you're looking for a month-to-month lease on some office space?"

"I am. As you know, my primary practice is with Parkman and Thornton in Boston, but because of some unusual circumstances here in Whitby, I'll be working on a case for a short, undetermined period of time. It would be preferable if the office were furnished."

Murphy leaned in and asked in a confidential tone, "This wouldn't have anything to do with the arrest of Katie Sullivan, would it?"

Titus realized his defense of the madam of a house of prostitution might not be taken well by the upright citizens of Whitby. "I'm sure you'll understand me when I say that client information is confidential."

"Oh, of course, of course." Murphy leaned away and assumed a more erect stance. "However, if I might, I want you to know that I would have no objection to renting you an office whoever your client is. We Irish have to stick together."

Titus couldn't keep his brows from rising at the statement. He himself wasn't Irish, so he had to assume Murphy was referring to Mrs. Sullivan. News spread fast in Whitby. He quickly recovered himself. "So, do you have an office that might be appropriate?"

"I think I do. If you'll follow me, I'll show it to you myself."

Brian Murphy led the way outside, then walked several yards along the sidewalk to the end of the building where a door was located. He pulled a key ring from his pocket, fingered through the keys until he found the one he wanted, then opened the door with it. A stairway led to the second floor.

Titus followed him up the stairs to a hallway lined with individual offices. Closest to the stairs was the office of an accountant. An insurance agent's office was across the hall.

Strong saw there were two more offices on either side as Murphy led the way to the rear. Lifting his key ring, he again sought the right key to open the office.

Inside there was a reception area with several chairs against one wall. A secretary's desk was to the left of a door to what Titus assumed was an inner office.

"It's a little spare, but as it's only temporary, I believe this should work for you."

"Can we see the private office?" Titus asked.

"Certainly." Murphy led the way and opened the door. He looked over his shoulder before entering and said, "There's a separate key for this door, but since the office is unoccupied, I usually don't lock it."

The private office was roughly the same size as the reception area. Instead of a secretary's desk, there was a larger executive desk with an office chair on wheels. The chairs in front of this desk were upholstered, and a couch was on the wall near the door. To the right, a small, round conference table was positioned in front of two empty bookcases. Filing cabinets lined the back wall on that side.

"I think this will do nicely," Titus Strong said. "What would you charge for it?"

Murphy named a sum significantly less than what Titus would have expected. He realized rents in Whitby were likely to be a lot lower than those in Boston, and from the looks of the doors off the main hall, most of the offices in this building were empty, an incentive to ask a low rent if Titus ever heard one.

"I'll take it. I'd like to occupy the office starting tomorrow morning, if that's agreeable."

Brian Murphy looked around him with a frown. "Well, I'd like to have it cleaned before you move in. I can try to get it done this afternoon, but I'm not sure that's possible. The cleaning staff usually comes in on weekends. If you don't mind a little dust, I suppose I could give you a key as soon as you sign the lease."

"I can handle the dust. I don't expect there to be anyone but myself using the office for a few days. Let's go sign that lease."

CHAPTER 19

It didn't take long for Titus to sign the lease and receive a set of keys to his new office. As long as he was out, he thought he'd take a walk to the marina and see if Joe Kelley was around. He knew the chances were slim, since it was past most people's lunchtime, and from what he knew of fishing, it was best to go early in the day. But he wanted to interview the potential secretary Tim Kelley had told him about as soon as possible. He wasn't sure when the preliminary hearing would be, but coming onto the case with no background was sure to result in a time crunch.

He was surprised, yet pleased, when he saw the Arvilla tied up at the dock and Kelley seated on the deck, a fishing net draped across his lap like a blanket.

"Joe!" he called out.

The old fisherman looked up from his task and smiled when he saw who'd called his name. "I'll be right there."

Kelley did something that looked very much like a woman stitching embroidery in her drawing room, but the device in his hand was much larger than a needle. After a few more passes, he slid the net off his lap and laid the device on top of it. He got up and came toward the dock.

"Come aboard." Kelley extended his hand to assist Strong onto the boat. "What brings you here today?"

Titus grunted as he dropped down onto the deck. "I thought you'd like an update on what's going on with Katie Sullivan."

"Aye. I would." Kelley looked him up and down. "Let's go fishing."

Titus looked down at his apparel, suitable for a lawyer in his official capacity, but not for getting fish guts on. "I'm not exactly dressed for a fishing trip. This won't take long."

"I think there are some clothes of Tim's down below that would fit you." The old fisherman's eyes locked on Titus's as he repeated with more emphasis, "Let's go fishing."

"Where would I find those clothes?" His stomach growled, reminding him he hadn't eaten since breakfast. He'd have to do without if the information the old fisherman wanted to impart was as important as his demeanor said it was.

"First cupboard on the right." Kelley headed toward the bowline and began to untie it. He paused and looked back over his shoulder with a grin. "If you're lucky, you might find some lunch in a chest in the bow."

Titus grinned back at him. He ducked his head as he went down the steps leading to the cabin. As expected, clothes more suitable for fishing than what he was wearing were in the cupboard, a pair of woolen trousers and a well-worn plaid shirt. He'd have to make do with his dress shoes. The trousers were about an inch short, but otherwise fit him perfectly. Once changed, he carefully folded his suit and shirt, and went looking for the chest.

As promised, it held sandwiches of coarse bread and large chunks of cheddar cheese. He passed on the one filled with cold fried fish. He emerged from below chewing on the first bite.

"Now you look like a real fisherman," Joe Kelley said. "Would you raise the jib and push the bow off while I take the tiller?"

Titus wasn't sure what the jib was, but remembering his previous fishing trip, he made an educated guess. After putting his sandwich down on one of the benches, he headed toward the front of the boat and raised the small sail there. Joe Kelley didn't curse at him, so he must have gotten it right. The old fisherman steered the boat into the harbor. Once they were clear of the marina, he said, "Now the mainsail."

Seeing as there was only one other sail on the sloop and it was larger than the jib, Titus felt more confident about raising that one. When he was done, he made his way back to where Kelley held the tiller.

"Not bad for a landlubber. You can finish your lunch now."

Titus stood a bit taller, and without willing it, his shoulders pulled back and he thrust his chest out. He located the remains of his sandwich, which had slid down the bench as the sloop heeled over. He brushed the dirt off the bottom of it as best he could and took another bite before taking a seat near Joe Kelley.

"Tim told me there was a classmate of his who was looking for a secretarial job."

"Aye. That would be Elisabeth Wade. She's spent the last few years nursing her father and so hasn't got any recent work experience, but Tim assures me she was at the head of her class."

"I hope her father has recovered sufficiently for her to take a full-time position." What Titus didn't need was a secretary who was constantly taking time off due to family matters.

The old fisherman shook his head. "Sadly, no. Tobias Wade passed toward the end of last year."

Titus wanted to slap himself for being a dolt. "I'm sorry to hear that. Does Miss Wade have a family of her own?"

"No, she never married." Kelley smiled. "Although Timmy has ofttimes wished that she would."

"Ah. But nothing in the immediate future, I assume."

"Not ever, from what I can tell. You know how it is. Sometimes the magic's there for only one person. From what I hear, Elisabeth hasn't ever felt the magic. More's the pity for poor Tim."

This was all well and good, but it was time to get to the point of this conversation. "Would you let her know I've found an office and would like to interview her tomorrow morning?"

"I can do that."

Titus gave him the address. But surely arranging a job interview wasn't what had prompted the insistence that he accompany Joe Kelley out on the water. It was time to find out what that was. "Isn't it time you told me the real reason?"

"What do you mean?"

"You know something you couldn't tell me back at the marina. I'm guessing it's because you didn't want anyone but me to hear it."

"Perhaps you should get a rod and the bait bucket and at least pretend to be fishing."

Titus raised his head and looked at the water around them. There were several other boats in the vicinity, any one of which could tell he wasn't fishing. And they might be suspicious of a charter fisherman who didn't have a fishing charter.

After locating a rod, baiting the hook, and casting the line out over the side, Titus asked, "Is this better?"

"You should learn to be more patient, man. Some things take time."

"All right," Strong said in a conciliatory tone. "I'm just curious as to what was so important I had to go on an impromptu fishing trip."

Bracing the tiller under his arm, the old fisherman pulled a pipe and tobacco pouch from his pocket. After filling the bowl and tamping down the tobacco, he traded the pouch for a box of matches, cupped his hands to block the wind while he struck a match and lit the pipe. He leaned back and closed his eyes as he drew in some smoke. After he'd breathed it out, he opened his eyes and said, "First, it's not a good idea to talk directly to Tim. He got a lecture from Morgan after your lunch last week."

"I had a feeling that was what happened as soon as Tim told me to talk to you. I'm sorry if I caused him trouble."

"It's nothing he can't handle. For now. But it wouldn't do for him to be seen palling around with a criminal defense attorney on a regular basis." He paused to let that sink in and smoked his pipe while Titus considered a response.

"Point taken." He thought he felt a pull on the line and turned his attention to his fishing for a bit. It didn't happen again. He must have imagined the tug. "Is there anything else?"

"There is. One night when Timmy was on patrol near Payne's Salvage Yard, he saw Tom Hinkle coming out with a knapsack slung over his shoulder. Just as he was about to confront Hinkle about it, old Nate Cooper beat him to it. They had some heated words. Timmy couldn't hear what they said, but the tone was clear. He saw Hinkle dig in his pocket and hand over a few bills to old Nate, who counted them, then smiled and nodded."

"So Hinkle paid Cooper to forget he'd seen him stealing from his employer."

"Well, I can't say that for sure, but you're not the only one to draw that conclusion."

"What did Tim do then?"

"Nothing. Tim's no fan of Ranson Payne, but he didn't think getting between him and one of his thugs would be healthy for him."

"Was it just the one time or does Hinkle regularly steal from the salvage yard?"

"I couldn't tell you. That was the one time Tim saw it, but it doesn't mean it never happened afterwards. Or before. What I do know is that Nate Cooper was suddenly drinking a much better brand of whiskey."

Titus paid attention to catching fish while thinking that piece of information over. He was sure Hinkle wouldn't like being blackmailed. The question was, was it a strong enough motive for murder?

CHAPTER 20

As Titus opened the door to his new office the next morning, he realized it felt right to be here, in this office, in this town. Leisure was all well and good for a week, maybe two. He could see where, under some circumstances, a month off would do a man good. But a man was meant for work, not lolling around, and he was definitely a man who needed a purpose in his life.

He'd stopped at a stationery store on Mayfield and picked up a pen, a bottle of ink, and a pad of paper. He wasn't sure what he'd be doing today, but whatever it was, making notes was certain to be a part of it. Another part of his job involved researching prior cases, but that would be difficult right now. He contemplated the empty bookcases and thought he should have brought back some of his law books when he went to Boston. He'd have to make another trip soon unless he could find a friendly local lawyer with a set he could borrow.

His first order of business should be to go to the courthouse and establish when the preliminary hearing was scheduled, but it was too early for that. If it was like most courthouses in the Commonwealth of Massachusetts, proceedings didn't get started until 10:00 AM, and while there were sure to be employees who arrived earlier, they'd likely be drinking coffee and catching up on gossip rather than wanting to deal with lawyers with questions.

"Mr. Strong?" a warm contralto sang from the doorway behind him.

Titus turned and saw an attractive woman with wide, honey-brown eyes, her dark hair pulled back from her face in some kind of bun. She carried a cardboard box awkwardly, almost dropping it.

He hurried over to take the box from her. Peering inside, he saw why she'd had a problem. The box contained a typewriter, pencils, pens, a stapler, a ream of typing paper, and a stenographer's notebook. "Miss Wade?"

"Yes. Thank you. I didn't realize how heavy the carton would get walking uphill."

"You walked?" he asked in a rising note of surprise. He couldn't imagine walking any distance carrying such a load, much less carrying it uphill.

When she smiled, her whole face glowed. "It was only from the trolley stop on Mayfield, just a block or two."

Titus put the carton on the small conference table. "I'd offer you some water, but I only just got here myself, and I came less prepared than you did." He already liked her, but he couldn't resist needling her a little. He stared pointedly at the carton. "You must be confident you'll get the job."

"I am. I'm fully qualified in clerical tasks, I'm available

immediately, and I don't think you have any other interviews scheduled," she said in a no-nonsense tone of voice.

"You're correct on the last point, and I'll have to take your word on the second one. Now let's see if the first is also true. If you'll take your stenographer's pad and a pencil and have a seat on one of the chairs in front of my desk, I'd like you to take a letter."

She efficiently retrieved her materials and sat where he'd asked her to. He really didn't have a particular letter he needed to be typed yet, but he'd dictated so many in the course of his career, it was easy enough for him to construct one on the spot. He didn't sit at his desk, preferring to think on his feet. He paced the length of the office and back as he spoke. "To Mr. Clive Waterstone," he began. Ten or fifteen minutes later, he concluded, "Yours respectfully, Titus Strong.

"Did you get all that?" he asked Elisabeth Wade.

"I did."

"Follow me." He hefted the box from the conference table and carried it to the secretarial desk in the outer office. He lifted the typewriter out of the box and placed it at the center of the desk in front of the chair. "Please transcribe the letter now. When you're finished, bring it to me."

"Very well," she said and opened the ream of paper, withdrew a few sheets, and put one in the typewriter. As she started the keys clacking away, Titus returned to his office.

She seemed businesslike enough. He had a feeling the letter would be perfect, but he wanted her to feel a little pressure. Lord knew, there'd be plenty of pressure if she took the job. He gazed out the window while he waited. A boy was throwing a ball to a dog in the yard across the street. A woman hung laundry on a clothesline next door. Everyday people doing everyday things. He wondered if his life would ever be called "everyday." Somehow, he doubted it. Even if it was, he was too much of an adventurer to live that way for long.

"Mr. Strong?" Elisabeth Wade called out for the second time today.

Titus turned from the window. She held a typewritten page in her hand. "You can put that on my desk, then have a seat while I look it over."

Titus strode across the room and sat down. He began reading the letter, matching it from memory to the words he'd dictated. As best as he could determine, Elisabeth Wade hadn't made a single error, either in her stenography or her transcription. He was impressed. "I see why you were confident you'd get the job. How soon can you start?"

"I'm ready to start right now."

"Good." He scanned the office, once again noticing how bare it was. "I think your first job should be to make a list of things we need. Don't forget a pitcher and some tumblers, things like that, as well as office supplies. Then go into town and order it all. I opened an account at the stationer's this morning." He reached in a pocket, took out his wallet, and withdrew several bills from it. As he handed them across the desk, he said, "This should take care of the sundries. If you need more money, tell them to deliver the goods and I'll pay for them then."

"Very well. Is there anything else I should do before I go?"

"Not just yet. I might have something for you this afternoon. Meanwhile, I need to go to the courthouse. I'll be back by lunchtime."

CHAPTER 21

Elisabeth, having neglected to ask Mr. Strong for fare for the trolley, walked along Mayfield Road to do her shopping. She had barely enough money in her pocket to pay for the trip back to the office. Fortunately, now that her typewriter and supplies were at the office, tomorrow she could ride her bicycle to work.

She first stopped at Nichols' Stationery and Office Supply store for the assorted materials they'd need: manila folders, pens and pencils, a pencil sharpener, carbon paper, baskets to organize paperwork, and paperclips. She then continued to the small general store, where she hoped to find a pitcher and a set of glasses and a teakettle, as well as tea and some biscuits. She'd noticed the small parlor-sized pot-bellied stove in the corner of Mr. Strong's office and thought it would be nice to have a hot drink once in a while.

As she was standing in the biscuit aisle trying to make up her mind as to which kind to buy, some clumsy person bumped into her, causing her to drop the package of biscuits she'd been holding. Elisabeth whirled around, intent on giving the oaf a tongue-lashing, but she only got as far as opening her mouth. She closed it when she saw who it was who had done the bumping.

"Amanda! I didn't know you were in town."

The full-figured woman seemed distracted. Her dirty-blonde hair was pulled back untidily with several wayward strands falling over a face that looked careworn and tired. "I only got here two days ago."

Sympathetically, Elisabeth said, "Of course. I imagine you came because of your father."

Amanda nodded. "I got on a train as soon as I got the telegram."

"Did your mother come with you?" Elisabeth bit her lip the minute the words were out of her mouth. She knew Amanda's parents were estranged, that her mother had taken Amanda with her to Richmond, Virginia, where she was from, years ago. Fortunately, Amanda Cooper didn't take offense.

"Oh, no. Mother passed last month."

"You poor dear! To have lost both parents in a month's time. You must be devastated." This didn't seem like the sort of conversation one would want to have in the middle of a grocery store. "I'm so sorry. I didn't know. Do you want to sit and have some lemonade and talk awhile?"

"Let me pay for the clothes I bought first."

Once the two women were seated in the small café with glasses of lemonade to slake their thirst, Amanda began. "A few months ago, Mother found out she had a cancer growing in her womb. It was quite advanced, and the only treatment was to remove all the organs affected." She cast her eyes down and focused them on the red candy-cane-striped straw she twirled in her fingers.

"That sounds very serious." What do you say when a friend's mother has had a disease that caused her death?

"It was. And we had no one to help us." She released the straw and wrapped her hands around the glass, her fingers tightening in a death grip. As she raised the glass to her lips, the muscles of her upper arm bulged with the tension that had spread upward from her hands. While Amanda Cooper might weigh more than the average woman, none of that weight was fat.

She remembered Amanda had been a champion swimmer in high school. "Are you still swimming?" Elisabeth asked, not wanting to dwell on the subject of her mother's illness even while casting about in her mind if there might be some way she could help.

"As often as I can. There's a swimming area at Forest Hill Park." A half-smile came to her lips. "I've even challenged the rapids in the James River a time or two."

"That sounds dangerous."

"It is. But I was swimming in the ocean from the time I could walk. After you've faced the swells from an off-shore hurricane in September, nothing else seems quite as challenging." The animation that had brightened her face when she talked of swimming faded. "Unless it's a fatal illness. And now this. I feel so helpless."

"Is there any chance your father may have left you something?" Elisabeth asked.

"I doubt it. He didn't own the keeper's cottage, since it belongs to the town. And I doubt he saved much from his earnings."

From what Elisabeth had heard of Nate Cooper, she had to agree with that opinion. "When was the last time you saw him?"

"Oh, it was years ago." Amanda stared out the window, as if seeing a memory. "Once we left Whitby, I never came back. He came to Richmond one time, Christmastime I think it was. He brought no presents, just himself looking for a room and a meal for the holiday."

"Isn't it possible he missed you and your mother?"

Amanda's gaze left the past and focused on Elisabeth. "I doubt it. Still, I would have liked to have seen him before he died. He was my father, after all."

"Would you ladies like to order lunch?" a waiter asked. He'd slipped into the space beside the table without either of the women noticing.

Horrified, Elisabeth asked, "Is it lunchtime already?" Her first day on a new job, and she'd spent an hour dallying with a friend when she should have been working. She could only hope Titus Strong wouldn't fire her before she'd barely begun.

"It is that, ma'am," the waiter said.

Elisabeth waved him off. "I'm sorry, Amanda, but I have to get back to work." She fumbled in her purse for the price of the beverage. "Will you be staying in town long?"

"Only long enough to arrange for my father's burial. I don't see why it's taking so long for the autopsy. From what I've heard of how he died, the reason was obvious."

"I don't know much about these things," *yet*, Elisabeth

mentally added, thinking that if all went well, she'd know a lot more by the time this case came to a conclusion. "But when it's an unnatural death, I'm sure they want to be thorough."

"Be that as it may, I don't want to spend any more time away from home than I have to."

CHAPTER 22

TITUS DRUMMED HIS fingers on his desk. Since Miss Wade hadn't returned from her errands yet, he had the office to himself. The clerk of the court had informed him Katie Sullivan's hearing was on the docket for 10:00 AM next Monday. Today was Tuesday. He was trying to figure out how he was going to build a defense in under a week.

He was convinced Katie hadn't murdered Nate Cooper, but there were no other suspects… except for, possibly, Tom Hinkle. If Nate Cooper was threatening to tell Payne about Hinkle's thefts, that could be a motive for murder. He imagined Payne wouldn't take the situation lightly. If the threats he'd seen the thug make was any indication, Hinkle might find himself with a bunch of broken bones. Or something worse.

And Katie still didn't have an alibi for the time of the murder. He was going to have to go to the Honey House and question her "girls." Even though she said none of them saw her, he wanted to confirm that for himself. It was possible she was trying to protect one—or all—of them from too close an examination by the police. She'd nearly said so herself.

"Good afternoon, Mr. Strong," a man's voice said.

Titus looked up to see a familiar face with a distinctive walrus mustache staring at him. "Campbell, isn't it?"

"It is." Owen Campbell straightened from his slouch against the frame of the doorway and came forward until he reached the chairs facing Titus. "I was wondering if you were in a trance." Without asking, he sat in a chair and stretched his long legs out in front of him, crossing them at the ankles.

"Something like that. I was trying to come up with a plan for all I have to do before next Monday." Titus realized he hadn't told anyone except Joe Kelley about his new office. "How did you know where to find me?"

"I'm a detective," Campbell said with a crooked grin.

"That's right. You work for Pinkerton, if I remember our conversation on the fishing boat rightly."

"Worked. I've been on my own for a while now. There aren't many good alternatives to being with the Pinkerton Detective Agency, but I've managed to pick up enough work to keep body and soul together. Speaking of which, would you happen to need some help?"

"Do you read minds as well as detect?" Strong asked.

"It doesn't take a mind reader to figure out one man isn't enough to put together a criminal defense in a situation like this."

Strong wanted to take him up on his offer, but he thought he should make one thing clear before he did. "So far, I'm doing this case pro bono. I've hired a secretary, but I wasn't planning on paying a detective out of my own pocket."

"Since it's only a week, and I'm on vacation, I'll consider it an adventure, something I'll be able to tell my grandchildren about," Campbell said with a wry smile. "If it goes longer than a week, we'll talk again."

"Good enough. Now let me tell you what I know about the case."

Strong ran through his sparse information quickly and finished with, "So far, since no one witnessed Katie Sullivan committing the murder, or even anywhere near the crime scene, I think we can cast reasonable doubt on her guilt by showing that Tom Hinkle also had a motive to kill Cooper. I'd like you to nose around, particularly at the salvage yard, and see if you can find anyone who knows more about that situation."

"That sounds easy enough. How about I come back here tomorrow morning with a report?"

"Good. We'll compare notes then and see where we stand." He rose from behind his desk and extended his hand.

Campbell unwound his legs and rose from his chair with the slinky movement of a snake uncoiling. The two men shook hands. Strong liked Campbell's firm grip and warm, dry skin. The feel of the handshake told him he was dealing with a man who was sure of himself, confident in his ability to do the job.

As they released their handshake, the sound of the door to the outer office opening announced the return of Elisabeth Wade. A few footsteps later, she appeared in the doorway to Titus's office carrying a shopping bag in each hand. Strong noticed Campbell's approving appraisal of his secretary. A twinge of jealousy tightened his gut. He silently told it to go away.

The Case of the Mysterious Madam

She took a few steps inside the office as she spoke. "Sorry to have taken so long, Mr. Strong. I ran into an old classmate, Amanda Cooper, in town. She's Nate Cooper's daughter, and we stopped to talk about her father's death. She's distraught, of course, and sorry she missed seeing her father alive..." Elisabeth Wade noticed Owen Campbell for the first time. "Oh, I'm sorry. I didn't know you were with someone."

"Miss Wade, I'd like you to meet Owen Campbell, former Pinkerton detective, who will be assisting with the investigation of our case."

"I'm pleased to meet you, Mr. Campbell."

"Owen," said the detective as he glided toward her and extended his hand.

Miss Wade hesitated a moment before putting down one of the shopping bags and taking it. Titus noticed that this time the detective didn't give the hand he held a vigorous shake, but did something more like a gentle squeeze.

"Shall we go down together?" Titus said to Campbell. "I'm going to do some investigating myself this afternoon."

Campbell nodded his head in acknowledgment.

"If I'm not back by five o'clock," Titus said to his secretary as he pulled a spare key off his key fob, "you can lock up and go home."

The two men left the office and headed down the stairs to the street.

CHAPTER 23

Titus smiled to himself as he walked up to the Honey House. Someone had hung baskets of yellow flowers around the perimeter of the porch, and a foot-tall sign depicting a honeybee in yellow and black was nailed on the white clapboard next to the door. He didn't remember seeing it the last time, but the way it showed signs of weathering told him it must have been there. He knocked three times rapidly.

Soon after, a woman with light brown hair cascading in waves to just below her shoulders answered the door. "Good afternoon. Welcome to the Honey House." Her voice was warm and welcoming. She opened the door wider and stepped back so he could enter.

"Good afternoon. I'm Titus Strong."

The woman looked puzzled.

"I'm Mrs. Sullivan's lawyer."

Her voice lost its seductive notes and turned businesslike.

"Oh, of course. What can I do for you, Mr. Strong?"

"I'd like to speak to each of the girls who works here," he said.

The voice that had started out so warm turned icy cold. "Why?"

"I'd prefer not to go into details. I want to find out what they remember from the night Nate Cooper was murdered, see if any of them could testify in Mrs. Sullivan's favor."

The woman closed the door, but she didn't lead him into the parlor. Titus wondered if the door would open again so she could throw him out. "I see. And how would you like to do this questioning?"

"Preferably, one at a time, in the parlor, if that's convenient."

"One at a time will cost you. For each one." Her eyes narrowed with suspicion. Or was it merely greed?

"You misunderstand me, Miss…"

"Sawyer. Linda Sawyer. I'm in charge when Mrs. Sullivan isn't available, and I don't think I do misunderstand you. I've dealt with lawyers before. Shysters, all of them. A fee isn't enough for them when dealing with women like us. Since they usually expect additional payment of a different kind, I'd prefer we get paid for whatever we're doing. It's our job."

This was getting difficult. "I'm afraid I can't pay you. That would have to come out of whatever the client is paying me, and as Mrs. Sullivan hasn't paid me anything, I have nothing to give in return. Surely we can come to some accommodation?"

Linda Sawyer looked thoughtful, then said, "I'll bring everyone to the parlor. You can ask your questions there, in front of me."

Titus started to sigh, then stopped himself. He didn't want to appear weak before this imperious woman. "As you wish, then. I'll wait in the parlor while you gather them for me."

Again he sat in one of the ivory and gold chairs, waiting. He hadn't imagined he'd encounter such opposition. Questioning the girls in a group had its disadvantages, not the least of which was that they'd be all too conscious of Miss Sawyer's presence. She would intimidate anyone.

Asking questions of a group also had a tendency for all of them to come up with the same responses. If one girl was sure enough in her answers, the others would give the same ones rather than being original and authentic.

In a few minutes, Linda Sawyer entered the parlor with five young women parading behind her. They settled themselves on the sofa and assorted chairs. Miss Sawyer remained standing in front of the window, where she had a good view of each of the women in the room.

Not being sure of what Miss Sawyer had told the girls, Titus decided an introduction was in order. "My name is Titus Strong. I'm representing Mrs. Sullivan in her preliminary hearing. I hope to gather enough evidence to arrange for bail so she can be released from jail. Hopefully, I can prove her innocence, but that might have to wait for the trial.

"I'd like to ask you some questions to see if one of you knows something that would help me do that."

He paused and took a look at each of the women in the room. Most of them were young, barely out of their teens. One appeared to be around thirty. He decided to start with her, thinking she'd be less intimidated than the others. He'd save Linda Sawyer for last. He looked at the thirty-year-old and smiled his most fatherly smile.

"Good afternoon, miss. Now, I just have a few questions for each of you. I want you to answer them as truthfully as you can. There aren't any right or wrong answers, so don't be afraid of giving a wrong one. Do you understand?"

"Yes, sir." Her hands fidgeted in her lap, clasping and unclasping, then smoothing the fabric of her skirt.

"Were you at the Honey House on the night of July second?"

"I was, sir. I'm here every night." She spoke in a matter-of-fact tone, her facial expression controlled and serious.

"Good." He smiled again in an attempt to put her at her ease. She tried to smile back. "Now, Mrs. Sullivan has told me she spent the evening in her room, working on her accounts. She claims not to have left her room during that time, but I'm wondering if she might have forgotten something simple, like going to get a glass of water or a cup of tea. Did you happen to see her at any time that evening?"

The woman frowned in concentration. The room was so quiet Titus could hear the ticking of the clock on the mantlepiece. Eventually, the frown smoothed out. "No, sir. I don't remember seeing her at all that night."

"Very well." He turned to the next girl, who had blonde hair tied with a blue ribbon that matched her eyes.

"What about you? Were you here on the night of July second?"

"Yes, sir. I don't have anywhere else to go."

"Did you see Mrs. Sullivan at any time that night?"

"No, sir," she answered quickly.

Too quickly, in Strong's opinion. Either someone had asked her the question before, or someone had prepared her for it.

"Take your time and think again. Are you sure you didn't see Mrs. Sullivan?"

Titus had to stifle a smile as her lips moved. He didn't have to be much of a lip-reader to see she was counting to ten. When she finished, she repeated her answer.

"I'm sure," she said. "I didn't see her that night."

All of the girls gave him the same answers, and he was beginning to think he'd wasted his time by coming here. There was just one more girl before he got to Linda Sawyer. He didn't hold much hope as he prepared to repeat his first question. "Emily, isn't it?"

"Yes, Mr. Strong."

"Were you here at the Honey House on the night Nate Cooper was murdered?"

"I was, Mr. Strong."

She didn't wait for him to ask the second question. "And I *did* see Mrs. Sullivan that night."

There was a quick intake of breath, and Titus Strong looked toward the sound. Linda Sawyer's eyes were wide, and she grasped the back of the sofa as if she were afraid of falling.

Defiantly, Emily went on. "I remember it clearly, because there weren't any customers because of the storm. I was reading a book in bed when I heard footsteps in the hall. I thought maybe some man had made his way here looking for… Well, what men usually come here for. So I opened my door, hoping maybe I could make a few coins, and saw Mrs. Sullivan coming out of her room." Her eyes focused on Strong's throughout her speech, steady and unyielding, leading him to believe she was telling the truth.

"'Go back to bed, Emily,' she told me. So that's what I did."

She flicked a defiant look in Linda Sawyer's direction.

Linda couldn't let the moment pass. "Emily! Mrs. Sullivan undeniably said she saw no one that night."

"I'm pretty sure she saw me," Emily said, her chin jutting out. "I know I saw her."

"Thank you, Emily," Titus said before Linda Sawyer could raise more objections. On the other hand, Katie *had* been firm about her statement. Emily might be lying in an attempt to protect the woman who had protected her from rape by Nate Cooper. Or possibly to please him. That worried him. "Are you sure enough of your memory to testify to it in court?"

Emily blanched. As he'd guessed, she hadn't thought about needing to repeat her statement in front of a judge.

"Emily?"

The girl swallowed, and in a voice much less sure than it had been a moment ago, said, "Yes."

CHAPTER 24

RATHER THAN GO back to his hotel, Titus decided he would stop back at his new office to make some notes while the interviews were fresh in his mind. As he'd expected, Linda Sawyer had answered his questions in a manner consistent with what Katie Sullivan had told him. Other than Emily, the women had presented a united testimony, a wall daring him to try to breach it.

He almost didn't recognize the office when he opened the door. Elisabeth Wade had transformed it from a bare space to an efficient workplace in a matter of hours. Her typewriter occupied a place of honor on the desk, and various office supplies had been arranged around it. A bouquet of flowers sat on the table between the chairs for waiting clients. She'd even hung a calendar from the local hardware store on the wall behind her.

She flashed him one of her bright smiles when she saw who

had entered. "Good evening, Mr. Strong. I didn't expect you back."

"I didn't expect to be back, but I thought I'd make some notes." He realized this would be a good time to make use of Miss Wade's secretarial skills. "Why don't you bring your stenographer's pad into my office, and I'll dictate them to you."

Her smile grew wider, and she picked up the pad and a pencil and followed him into the executive office. Here, too, she had worked her magic. His desk had also been fitted out, a tray with a pitcher and glasses sat on the small conference table, and a teapot was on top of the stove. Typical a woman. He'd have to see about getting a coffeepot, since that was his preferred beverage.

He settled into the chair behind his desk and tented his fingers. As soon as she'd taken her place in one of the chairs in front of him, he started speaking. When he was done, he lowered his hands to the arms of his chair and asked, "Did you get all that?"

"Yes, I did. I'll type them up for you right away." She began to rise from her chair, then sank back down as he spoke.

"It can wait until the morning. I assume you're as tired and hungry as I am after working all day."

"I am, a little. But I enjoyed it."

"We'll see if you still enjoy your job after a couple of weeks. I have a feeling things might get intense around here."

"I don't mind hard work." She used her pencil to do something in the margins of her stenographer's pad.

Titus raised his head and tried to peer at what she'd written. It didn't look like words, or even Pitman, more like little doodles, swirls, and something that looked like a flower.

She caught him looking at what she'd done and blushed. "It's a habit I have when I'm thinking."

He smiled at her. "And what were you thinking about?"

"Didn't you find it odd that only"—she consulted her notes—"only Emily claimed to have seen Mrs. Sullivan on the night of the murder?"

"You noticed that?"

She nodded. "Of course. The rest of the women told the same story, in lockstep as it were, which is even odder."

"Go on."

"Emily is the one who Nate Cooper tried to attack at the hotel, right?" When Titus nodded, she continued, "Well, she might feel she owed something to the woman who saved her from that fate. I can't help but wonder if Emily wasn't saying she saw Mrs. Sullivan in order to protect her."

"The same thing crossed my mind." Titus liked the way Miss Wade thought for herself. The secretaries he'd dealt with in Boston never had any opinions, or if they did, they kept them to themselves. Everything was "Yes, sir" and "No, sir" and "Very good, sir." This was much better. "Was there anything else you were thinking about?"

Her expression became very serious. "Of course, there's another explanation. Maybe everyone else was lying."

"Why would they do that?" Titus asked. "That wouldn't benefit Mrs. Sullivan at all."

"I don't know. But women in that profession are likely to have a lot of secrets they don't want generally known." Her faced pinked up again. "Many of them they wouldn't want to talk to a man about."

"I hadn't thought about that. I wonder if Owen Campbell

knows any female detectives who could approach the residents of the Honey House. I'll have to ask him when he comes in tomorrow."

Miss Wade's eyes sparkled, and her voice almost sang as she said, "He's coming in tomorrow? I'll make sure we're ready for him, then."

Titus's eyes strayed to the teakettle. "Having some coffee wouldn't be amiss."

Her eyes followed his. "Oh, I'm sorry. I didn't think… I'll stop on my way in tomorrow and pick up a pot and some coffee beans."

"I think that's it, then." Titus hesitated. Should he invite her out to dinner? It was past suppertime by at least an hour. Then he remembered his wife in Boston. It wouldn't be proper for a married man to be seen with an unmarried woman. Not that there was anyone in Whitby who would think to tell her. But Whitby was a recreational town, and filled with vacationers down from the city. You never knew who you'd run into. "I'll see you tomorrow morning."

"Have a good night." Elisabeth Wade picked up her things and left his office. He sat behind his desk for several minutes after her heard the outer door close. Then he rose from his chair, locked first his office, then the outer office, on his way out, and slowly made his way back to the Seaview Hotel.

CHAPTER 25

THE AROMA OF fresh-brewed coffee wafted toward him as Titus opened the office door. A smile lit up his face, even though he'd had two cups with his breakfast. As far as he was concerned, you could never have too much coffee. It was the fuel that powered the brain and lifted the spirit. His pleasure must have shown on his face.

"If I'd known a cup of coffee would transform you from a lion into a pussycat, I would have bought a coffeepot sooner," Miss Wade said.

"Don't let your eyes deceive you. Enough caffeine and you'll see the lion again, ready to pounce."

Her laugh warmed his soul, but was quickly replaced by the demeanor of a business-minded secretary. "Mr. Campbell is waiting in your office," she said.

"Thank you. Would you fetch me a cup of coffee while I get settled in?"

"Of course." Miss Wade led the way into the private office and headed for the coffeepot on the pot-bellied stove, while Titus went to greet the detective.

"You've gotten an early start," Titus said as he settled into his chair.

"A man can't let the grass grow under his feet, especially when there's a court date." Owen Campbell picked up his coffee cup and drank deeply, then held it out to Elisabeth as she arrived with Strong's coffee. "Might I have another cup?"

"Certainly."

"After you've gotten Campbell's coffee, and some for yourself if you like, please get your notebook. I want to document everything on this case." He tested the coffee and found it to his liking. Not only could Elisabeth Wade take shorthand, she made an excellent cup of coffee. Several typewritten pages sat in front of him. "I'll be with you in a minute, Owen," Titus said as he picked up the sheets and read through them quickly. Miss Wade's typing skills were on a par with all her other skills. He'd been lucky to find her.

By the time he'd finished reading, the secretary had returned with her pad and pencil and seated herself in the other chair in front of his desk.

"Are you ready?" Titus asked the detective.

"Always." He pulled a notepad from his pocket and referred to it before starting. "You were right about the salvage yard. I got chummy with one of the workers there, a Fred Stevens, who was all too willing to give me the scuttlebutt on Tom Hinkle, among other people. He knew all about Hinkle stealing from the salvaged goods." He paused for more coffee.

"Hinkle knew when they'd brought back something of value

from one of the wrecks offshore and regularly used a break in the fence to steal some of it at night. He had a good thing going until Nate Cooper stumbled by," he looked up from his notes to add, "and I mean literally stumbled. Old Nate had a fondness for drink." He looked back down before continuing. "Cooper threatened to tell Ranson Payne about the thefts unless Hinkle cut him in for a share of the proceeds. Rather than take a chance on having a fatal accident, something Payne has been known to arrange before, Hinkle paid Cooper to keep his mouth shut."

"So Nate Cooper *was* blackmailing him. I wonder if there were any others." Titus worried his lip as he considered how they might locate other blackmail victims, if they existed.

"Did you have anyone in mind? I can't exactly walk down Mayfield Road stopping random passersby to ask them if they've been blackmailed."

Strong shook his head. "Unfortunately, no. But it's been my experience that a blackmailer usually has more than one victim."

"There's more," Campbell said, getting Titus's attention. "Did you ever wonder why there are so many shipwrecks off the coast of Whitby?"

"I assumed it had to do with the way the peninsula juts out into the harbor. There's also a sandbar offshore that's got to be a hazard to navigation."

Campbell nodded. "Yes, that's why the lighthouse was built —to warn passing ships of the shallow water and the rocks off the point."

"But the light was out during the storm," Titus said.

"Now you're getting it. It seems as if the light is often out when there's a rich cargo due to pass by. Through his connections, Payne has advance notice of things like, oh, barrels of Kentucky's finest bourbon being onboard. He makes sure the lighthouse keeper has a problem with the light on those nights."

"You're saying Nate Cooper was instructed to douse the light by Payne?"

"Well, not directly. He sends Hinkle to do his dirty work for him."

Titus raised an eyebrow. "Curiouser and curiouser, said Alice."

"Isn't it?" Campbell picked up his cup and tilted his head back, downing what remained inside before continuing. "According to my source, Hinkle went out there the night of the murder to deliver Payne's message. He just so happened to be carrying Katie Sullivan's derringer, which he'd picked up after she dropped it during that ruckus at the hotel.

"For some reason, Cooper didn't want to comply. The two got into a heated argument, and Hinkle shot Cooper, who dropped, unconscious, to the floor. Hinkle made sure the light was out himself and left."

"That's great news!" Titus said. "Will your source testify to that at the hearing?"

"I got the feeling that he only heard what Hinkle told him. He wasn't actually present when it happened." Campbell went to pick up his coffee cup again and stopped, remembering it was empty.

"Would you like more coffee, Mr. Campbell?" Elisabeth Wade asked sweetly.

"No, thank you. Any more and I'll be jittery all day."

"So it would be hearsay evidence," Titus said, disappointed.

Campbell nodded. "And to top it off, Hinkle says in his rush to get out of the keeper's cottage, he left the gun behind, meaning someone else could have shown up afterwards and used it to kill Cooper."

"But wasn't Cooper dead already?" Strong asked.

"Not according to Hinkle. Hinkle swears Cooper was breathing when he left the lighthouse."

Strong tented his fingers as he thought. "I wonder why Cooper was so reluctant to keep the lighthouse dark that night. From what you've told me, he was cooperative every other time."

"Should I try to talk to Hinkle and find out if Cooper gave him a reason?"

"If you can do it without raising too much interest on Ranson Payne's part." Titus went back to his ruminations.

"Are we done now?" Campbell asked.

He'd almost forgotten there were other people in the room. "Sorry. I was trying to think if there was anyone else with a motive to kill Nate Cooper. We know Katie Sullivan vowed revenge for the way he treated Emily. Hinkle was being blackmailed, which gave him a motive. Let's see… What are other reasons one person would kill another? I don't think jealousy comes into play. Somehow I can't picture Cooper being part of a love triangle. Or that anyone would want the keeper's job that badly. There might be another blackmail victim, but we've already figured out that would be tough to confirm. There's always greed. It's amazing how many people will kill if they see a profit in it." He stopped as he remembered something, then opened the middle drawer of his desk and grasped the piece of eight he'd found near Cooper's body.

Titus put his fist on the desk top. "I don't want this talked about outside of the three of us." He looked first at Campbell, who nodded, then Miss Wade, who looked puzzled, but finally nodded as well. He opened his fist and extended his hand, palm up, so they could see. "You know what this is?"

"It looks like a tarnished piece of silver," Elisabeth Wade said.

"It is," Titus said. "But it's more than that."

"Could I see it a minute?" Campbell asked. Titus dropped the wedge-shaped item into Campbell's hand. The detective looked at it closely, turned it over and examined the other side. "Don't tell me this is part of that pirate treasure?"

"I don't know," Strong said. "It's definitely a piece of eight. Tim Kelley told me the odd coin and pieces of eight often wash up on shore, especially out at the Point. He didn't seem to think that meant there really was a mythical pirate treasure to be found. But what if Nate Cooper came upon, if not a treasure chest, a significant number of gold and silver coins?"

"That will be as tough to find out as who else Cooper might have been blackmailing," Campbell said. "I doubt if he kept his hoard in the cottage. Or if he did, how we'd manage to search for it. There's a new keeper out there now."

"I heard. Ranson Payne's nephew," Titus said. "He can't be there all the time. He has to come into town for supplies occasionally. I wonder if he's fond of gambling or, ummm, other entertainments. I'll have to ask Mrs. Sullivan the next time I see her." He avoided looking at Elisabeth. While she hadn't been particularly disturbed when he'd talked about visiting the Honey House, he didn't feel it was proper to discuss prostitution in front of a lady.

Campbell said, "Let me nose around a bit and see if I can figure out a time when the keeper's cottage will be unoccupied."

CHAPTER 26

Titus placed the weekly newspaper on his desk and looked longingly at the coffeepot on the cold stove. It was too early for Miss Wade to be in, and he wasn't sure if he remembered how to start a fire. He was sure he had no idea of how to make coffee. One of the handicaps of being a member of the wealthy class was that you didn't do a lot of things for yourself. There were always servants around to take care of daily tasks for you.

Checking his watch, he saw it shouldn't be more than fifteen minutes until his secretary arrived, and so he began to read the account of the shipwreck that had taken place only ten days ago. An overview of the disaster had appeared in last week's paper, but this week's article was a series of interviews with the survivors and rescuers, which was of more interest to Titus.

The head of the lifesaving team boasted of the heroism displayed by his men, recounting how one of the lifeboats had almost capsized, and how several passengers had been ducked under the waves while riding the breeches buoy to shore. Titus thought that must be the name of the device he'd seen used to fetch people off the sinking ship.

A female survivor described how terrified she was when she'd been washed overboard and left to flounder in the roiling seas. She told a tearful tale of a mother dying in Richmond, Virginia, and how she'd come to New England to try to reunite with her father. He froze as he came to the sentence with her name. He read it again, just to make sure he'd read it right.

Just then, there was a rap on his doorframe. He looked up to see the old fisherman standing awkwardly in the doorway.

"Joe!" he said. "I would have thought you'd be out on your boat by now."

"I've already been out to check my lobster pots. It's a little early for the tourists to be signing on for a fishing charter yet." He glanced furtively over his shoulder. "Do ye mind if I shut the door?"

Wondering why Kelley was being so secretive, Titus said, "Go ahead, although I'm not expecting anyone this morning except my confidential secretary."

Joe Kelley stepped inside and shut the door behind him. He shuffled over to Strong's desk and sat in a chair without asking permission. "How is the case going?"

"Not as well as I'd like. Mrs. Sullivan doesn't have a solid alibi for the time of the murder, and the killer used her derringer. I don't know enough about this town to come up with another suspect with a stronger motive than she had. But I still have a few days, and I've hired Owen Campbell to do some detective work."

"Is that the Pinkerton that was on my charter?"

Titus nodded.

"He must be expensive." Kelley jammed a hand in his pocket.

Titus heard a muffled clinking sound, but didn't think much of it as he focused on whether to tell the old fisherman that both he and Campbell were working for free. In the end, he decided to keep that to himself. It wouldn't do for the town to know they could get his services, which carried a hefty price in Boston, for nothing. A picture of dozens of poor folks lined up at his door looking for something for nothing formed in his mind. "I'm not worried about the money at this point. Mrs. Sullivan and I will settle up after she's proven innocent."

"You're that confident, then?"

He wasn't, but he didn't want to admit his misgivings. "Is that all you came here for this morning? To find out how the case was going?"

"No." Kelley pulled a fist out of his pocket and rested it on Strong's desk. "I've been thinking you should be paid. Men work harder when they're getting paid. The better they're paid, the more motivated they are to do a good job."

Titus glanced down at the fist.

"Aye," Joe Kelley said as he opened his fingers and revealed the five gold coins lying in his palm. "I've brought you something in payment."

He felt his eyes bulge. "Are those…" his voice caught, and he stopped to clear his throat. In a more assertive tone, he asked, "Are those Spanish doubloons?"

"They are. And I'd appreciate it if you didn't noise it about where you got them. I would have changed them for cash myself, but if I walked into the bank here, there'd be a riot. I was thinking you could exchange them in Boston, quiet-like, where they might not draw as much attention."

"I'm afraid they'll draw attention no matter where they're exchanged or sold." Titus picked up his pen and tapped it on his desk while he thought. There was one place that might do. "Tell me. Is the story of the pirate treasure true then?"

Kelley gave him a gap-toothed grin. "It might be. Or it might not. Depends on how many other cases you'll be taking on in Shipwreck Point."

"Oh, I'm sure this will be the only one." Even as the words came out of Titus's mouth, he wondered if they were true.

One at a time Kelley put the gold doubloons on Titus Strong's desk. "As soon as you put those out of sight, I'll be going about my business."

Titus took the hint and scooped up the coins. He pulled a handkerchief out of his pocket and wrapped them inside before putting the bundle in his pocket, remembering the clink he'd heard when they were in Joe Kelley's. As good as his word, Kelley rose from his chair and headed for the door.

As soon as he'd left the office, Elisabeth Wade came in. "What was Mr. Kelley doing here?"

"I'd rather not say." He gave her a warm smile. "I'm so glad you're here now. I much prefer your company to the old fisherman's."

A warm flush suffused her cheeks, and he realized that his statement could have more than one meaning. The back of his neck felt hot. He hoped the warmth wouldn't spread to his face. Quickly he added, "How soon will the coffee be ready?"

Was that disappointment he saw on her face? Or relief?

CHAPTER 27

TITUS HUNG BACK as the ferry pulled into Long Wharf. Addison Slater, who'd been on the first fishing trip with Joe Kelley, had hurried toward the exit as they approached the pier. Titus hadn't seen him since that day. He'd assumed Slater had gone back to Boston after the holiday, if he'd thought about him at all.

But now, with five gold doubloons in his pocket, he didn't want to take a chance on meeting up with the man, who'd shown an inordinate interest in the pirate treasure yarn. In fact, the sooner he exchanged the coins for cash, the happier he'd be.

Once he was sure Slater was well on his way, Titus followed the crowd down the ramp. A line of hansom cabs waited with hopes of picking up a fare from the ferry passengers. He hurried to engage the first one. "First National Bank," he said, then climbed inside.

When he arrived at the bank, Titus didn't waste time, but went directly to the office of Hanley Barrett, the vice president who handled his accounts.

"Mr. Strong," Barrett's assistant gushed. They always gushed when you had money. "So nice to see you again. Would you like to speak with Mr. Barrett this morning?"

"If he's available." Titus didn't know what he'd do if Barrett wasn't available. He hoped he wouldn't have to deal with that circumstance.

"Let me check." The man scurried down a nearby hallway.

"Go right in," the assistant said when he returned a minute later.

"Good morning," Barrett said heartily as he shoved out his hand. "Glad to see you again. Mrs. Barrett and I saw Victoria the other night, and she told me she was headed for Newport this week. Are you going to accompany her or do you have another important case to defend?"

Titus felt that the banker was asking for too much personal information, but since they often met socially, he didn't want to seem standoffish. "I'm afraid it's the latter, Barrett."

"Too bad, too bad." The banker gestured toward a chair and sat behind his desk. "What can I do for you this morning?"

Titus had worked out his story while riding over on the ferry. "I have a client who's inherited a few Spanish doubloons from a distant relative and is looking to exchange them for cash."

Barrett's eyebrows shot up at the mention of the doubloons. "I'd recommend you sell them at auction. That's where you'd get the best price."

"I mentioned that to my client, but he's shy of publicity and would prefer that it not become publicly known that he had the coins. No, I was hoping you'd be able to give me a fair price for them. The bank could then auction them off discretely. Even if anyone discovered that First National was the consignor, there'd be no personal interest in a bank, seeing as they deal in all sorts of money."

Barrett leaned back in his chair and closed his eyes for a moment. When he opened them, he said, "Why don't you let me ask around a bit, and I'll get back to you next week."

Strong's heart sank. Taking a deep breath, he reached in his pocket and brought out the doubloons, laying them on the desk in plain view. "I was hoping to make the exchange now. You see, my client is short of cash, and as long as he's short, so am I, if you know what I mean."

Barrett had been staring intently at the five shiny gold coins ever since Titus had laid them on his desk. He raised his head to meet Strong's gaze. "Ah." He closed his eyes briefly again. "In that case, I would be willing to give you one hundred dollars now. That would be the value of the gold. I would anticipate that the auction price for the coins would be higher, but it's impossible to know how much higher until they're sold."

Torn between wanting to be rid of the coins and wanting a fair price for them, Titus said, "I've got another idea. How about I sell them to you for one hundred dollars now, and if they sell at auction for over one hundred dollars, I get fifty percent of that."

"That sounds fair enough. Let me have Gerald type up a bill of sale."

A short time later, the assistant brought in the document, plus two carbon copies, and Strong and Barrett signed all three copies. Barrett filled out a draft for one hundred dollars and handed that to Titus with his copy of the sales agreement. "You can cash this at any teller window."

"It was good doing business with you," Titus said as he rose to his feet.

"And with you, as always," Barrett replied.

Titus left Barrett's office and headed to the row of teller cages. He jumped at the sound of a voice behind him.

"Strong, isn't it?"

Titus turned and found Slater behind him. He couldn't help but wonder if he'd been followed. He forced a smile to his lips and answered, "Yes. You were on that fishing charter I took over in Whitby, weren't you?"

"I was." The man extended his hand. "Addison Slater."

"That's right, I remember now. Good seeing you again." He pointedly continued on his way to cash the draft, but he felt a hot spot in the middle of his back, as if Slater's stare was burning a hole in his jacket.

CHAPTER 28

Titus made sure Slater was occupied at a teller window before he left the bank. There were some other stops he wanted to make before catching the ferry back to Whitby. He didn't want to be followed to the location of the first one.

He caught one of the electric streetcars to Park Square, from which he took another one down Tremont Street to his destination. The South End was a mixture of tenements for immigrant families and cheap rooming houses. It also happened to be where Titus Strong grew up.

Out of habit, he kept his head low. Being of English descent in the predominantly Irish neighborhood had meant suffering from the rowdy gangs that roamed the streets in those days. While he didn't expect to be waylaid by a gang of toughs at this time of day at his current age and size, habits die hard.

Just as he was about to knock on the door of a run-down tenement, it opened and vomited forth a grungy man with a day's worth of stubble sprouting on his chin. The man, who was securing his trousers, gave Titus a knowing wink. "She's all yours."

He fought back the urge to punch the man in the face.

A woman stood on the other side of the room, facing away from him as she rearranged her hairpins in front of a cracked mirror. Her disheveled, once raven-black hair was now streaked with gray. "I'll be with you in a minute."

When she turned, her face lit up with a smile. "Titus! I'm so glad to see you. It's been a long time."

Anger still seethed in his gut. "Mother, I've told you before you don't have to do this. I send you money every month. If it's not enough, I'll send you more."

"Don't be so quick to get on me about the way I make my living. I raised you from what I earned on my back. It paid for your law school."

"And I appreciate it," he said sincerely. "But it's dangerous to have strange men in the house. How many times has one taken his hand to you?"

"Too many," she admitted. "But I can stand it. Your father was worse. Would you like some tea?"

She asked it in the same way one of Victoria's friends would have invited you to tea in her grand parlor. Grand didn't describe this shabby room with the threadbare carpet and a worn coverlet over the much-used bed. "What about the diseases?"

"I'm careful about that. I think I'll put the kettle on." She turned and filled one with some water from a pitcher and lit the gas on the small stove that stood in the corner of the room.

Titus sighed. His mother was as proud and independent as he was. He wouldn't be surprised to learn that she'd taken all the money he'd sent her and put it aside in case he needed it.

While the tea was brewing, his mother plied him with questions. "And how is life treating you up in that big townhouse you live in?"

"I haven't been living there lately," he admitted. "In fact, I've been summering in Whitby."

"Whitby, is it? What made you go to that den of iniquity? Perhaps you take after your mum after all."

Titus gave her a wry smile. Leave it to his mother to know that kind of thing. "I didn't know it was a den of iniquity when I chose it. I just remembered the fun times we had when we went to the seashore for a day. I was particularly fond of the cotton candy you bought me."

She poured the tea into two large mugs. He noticed the one she chose for herself had a crack in it. "How long do you plan on staying there?"

"I'm not sure exactly. I'm currently defending a woman for murder."

"Is that what you call a vacation?"

He barked a laugh. "I don't suppose it is, but it's something I felt I needed to do as long as I was vacationing there." He smiled.

"I think I prefer my kind of whorin'."

Titus had long since ceased to be shocked by his mother's vocabulary, if he ever was. "This is different. It's not like the Richard Davenport case. I think this client really is innocent."

"Well, I'll leave that up to you. And how is Victoria?"

"She's gone off to Newport for the summer."

"Is it worth it, Titus?" Her voice was filled with gentleness and concern.

"I'm not sure, mother. When I married Victoria, I thought she was everything I'd ever want in a woman. Over time, I've come to think there might be something more to a marriage than what she and I have." For a minute, an image of him sharing a home with Elisabeth Wade flashed through his mind. She was smiling. So was he. He shook his head to clear it. "Regardless, I made my decision, and I'm honor-bound to stand by it."

He pulled out his watch and was alarmed at how late it had gotten. "I'm sorry, mother. I'm going to have to hurry if I want to catch the ferry back to Whitby." He put down his mug and rose to his feet. Bending down to kiss her cheek, he said, "I'll try to come to visit you more often."

"I know you'll try, son. But you have your own life now. I'll understand if you don't have time for Southie anymore. Or me."

"I'll always have time for you."

CHAPTER 29

As the ferry approached the Whitby dock, Titus hefted the case weighted with law books from where it was sitting at his feet. He'd stopped at his house in Boston and packed up a selection from his personal library after visiting his mother. Fortunately, Victoria had already left for Newport, so he didn't have to contend with her complaints.

He had to wrestle the heavy box down the gangplank on his own. A sardonic smile came to his lips. If he stayed in Whitby, he'd have to get in better shape. He'd grown soft sitting behind a desk. As he lumbered toward the stand where hansom cabs waited, his breathing became labored. He'd definitely have to see about taking up some kind of activity, perhaps that new game of tennis that was all the rage. He wondered if his club would build a court for the members to use. Fortunately, it didn't take long for him to engage a hansom cab to transport him to his hotel, where a bellboy took the box and carried it up to his suite for him.

He had no time to spare if he wanted to be prepared for his case on Monday. He sat at the desk and tapped his pen on a legal pad as he thought. He decided to make two lists.

"Pro:" he wrote at the top of one page. Beneath this, he wrote:

1. No one saw Katie Sullivan at the lighthouse on the night of the murder.
2. Cooper had been blackmailing Hinkle.
3. There might be more blackmail victims.
4. There was the unnamed source who said Hinkle had Katie's gun and shot Cooper with it.
5. Could Hinkle be persuaded to testify?

Flipping the page, he wrote "Con:" at the top of the next one.

1. Katie Sullivan threatened Nate Cooper in view of witnesses, including Tom Hinkle.
2. Her derringer was unquestionably the murder weapon.
3. She had no alibi for the time of the murder.
4. From what Owen Campbell said, the unnamed source could only provide hearsay evidence.

He wasn't sure he had enough to prove reasonable doubt, particularly if the judge was one of Ranson Payne's cronies. Something told him Payne was behind this, even though he had no concrete proof of that. Would a bribe affect the outcome? He wasn't sure why Ranson Payne would want to put Katie Sullivan in prison. Was it only to keep his henchman out of jail?

He had to assume the prosecutor, Edgar Garner according to the paperwork he'd gotten, would call the witnesses from the hotel confrontation. Since Titus had also witnessed this event, he didn't see a way to turn the facts around to *not* point to Katie Sullivan. No, he'd have to rely on discrediting the other witnesses and hope that would be enough.

Too agitated to sleep, Titus entered Golden Chances in search of a poker game. Not one in which Ranson Payne was playing. It didn't take long to find a table that had an available chair. The feel of the cards as he slid them into his hand and the sound of the ball ratcheting around a roulette wheel nearby comforted him. Here, he was in his element. His mood improved in direct proportion to the size of the stack of cash in front of him. He hadn't lost his touch after all.

"I should have known I'd find you here," Owen Campbell's voice said from over his shoulder.

"I didn't know you were looking for me." Titus put a couple of cards face-down on the table and held up two fingers toward the dealer.

"I didn't want to leave a message anywhere."

Titus glanced up in an attempt to read what that meant on Campbell's face. The former Pinkerton was too good at disguising his thoughts.

Titus picked up the two new cards the dealer had dealt and contemplated his options. He stood a good chance of winning this hand, but it was more important to win Katie Sullivan's case. He collapsed the fan of cards and placed it on the table. "Fold. Thank you, gentlemen, for a most enjoyable game. Perhaps we can play again some other time."

A gloomy man across from him, his cheeks sunken into his gray face, scowled at Titus. "Maybe next time you'll give us a chance to win our money back."

Titus smiled ingratiatingly at the complainer as he gathered up his cash. "Perhaps."

"Shall we take a walk outside?" Titus said as he joined the lanky man who had commanded his attention.

Campbell nodded and the two men exited the gambling room in silence. "Let's go down to the water," Campbell said when Titus started to turn right on the boardwalk.

Titus raised his eyebrows. "All right." He altered the direction of his steps and followed the detective down the stairs to the sand.

Campbell stopped just inches from where the waves splashed on the beach. The sound of the surf covered the noise of the gaming that leaked out of the hotel. When the detective opened his mouth to speak, Titus had to lean closer to hear the words he was saying.

"I spent yesterday getting acquainted with several of the residents of the town of Whitby," Campbell said.

He had Titus's attention now. "Anyone in particular?"

"Oh, various shopkeepers and those who sell souvenirs and food to the tourists. While I was out, just fishing for information in general, I also ran into Officer Barney Bailey, a rotund gentleman with little chance of advancement."

"What do you mean?"

"Let's just say he'll not get into Harvard University any time soon. He spends a lot of time on the night shift, patrolling the streets of Whitby after dark."

"You say that like it's significant." The detective had piqued Strong's curiosity. He wished Campbell would get to the point.

"He was working the night shift the night of the storm.

Complained about it quite a lot. With a little 'tea' and sympathy, he admitted to keeping a particular eye on the Honey House that night."

Now Titus was more than curious. "What did he see?"

"Nothing much there." Campbell paused, as if enjoying the suspense.

"Get on with it, man!"

"It was out toward the Point where he noticed something. There's a long stretch of what the rich call 'cottages,' mansions to you and me, strung along the beach between here and Shipwreck Point, and Bailey is charged with keeping an eye out for burglars in that area in particular. Many of the owners only come for a few weeks in the summer, leaving the homes vacant a good part of the year."

"What has that to do with our investigation?"

"While patrolling that section of town, Bailey was amazed to see Mrs. Katie Sullivan riding by on her bicycle. He didn't know she made house calls." Campbell chuckled.

"So she might have an alibi after all."

"It appears as if she might. But I don't think she'd be willing to ask her rich client to testify for her. The scandal would be such that none of the swells would ever pay for her services again. In fact, her client, whoever he might be, might make sure she was charged with prostitution, and the Honey House shut down, if she let it became known."

Titus furrowed his brow. "Which is why she refuses to tell anyone where she was that night and claims she was closeted in her room."

"There's another possible explanation," Campbell said. "What if she was returning from the lighthouse?"

CHAPTER 30

Titus set the carton of law books on the floor and inserted his key in the office door. When he turned it, there was no resistance from the tumblers. He was surprised to find the door unlocked, but the sound of typewriter keys clacking away reassured him.

He opened the door. "Good morning, Miss Wade. You're in early."

She looked up and gave him a smile that made him feel as if he was basking in the sun in a lounge chair on the beach.

"I want to be ready. Today will be my first time taking notes in court."

He lifted the box of books to his shoulder and entered the office. She leaped from her seat to open the door to his private office for him. "Thank you," he said as he put the carton on the small table. He lifted the flaps, exposing the law books inside. "When you have a chance, would you put these in the bookcase?"

Miss Wade peered inside. "Do they go in any particular order?"

"Well, you can see the volume numbers on the spine, but I only brought a few select books from my collection, those that had cases I thought might be applicable to ours, so for now order isn't important."

"I'll do that as soon as I get the coffee started for you." She turned to get the pot.

"Never mind. I'm not staying. I have to consult with Mrs. Sullivan before the hearing." When he saw the puzzled look on her face, he knew he had to tell her the problem. "Last night, I learned there was a witness who saw her riding her bicycle out near Shipwreck Point the night of the murder. I need to know if that witness was lying. Or if she was when she said she spent the night in her room."

"That sounds serious."

"It is. Too often clients lie to their lawyers, afraid something will put them in a bad light. But it makes it harder to defend them if you don't know the truth. Clients should always tell their lawyers the truth. Let the lawyers do the lying." He grinned. "Meet me at the courthouse at five to nine. We'll go in together."

The rotund police officer at the front desk at first gave Titus a hard time about seeing Katie Sullivan. From his girth, Titus thought this must be Barney Bailey, the officer Campbell had told him about. If what Campbell had told him was true—and he had no reason to doubt the former Pinkerton detective, it wouldn't take much to intimidate him. Strong asked to speak to Chief Morgan, and the officer suddenly changed his mind.

After a much shorter wait than he'd experienced the first time, the officer brought Katie into the interrogation room. She was dressed in a modest shirtwaist, something suitable for court. Her demeanor was somber. No smiles or teases this morning, which was totally appropriate, given Titus's reason for being there.

"Sit down, Mrs. Sullivan," he said as he did the same. "I received some disturbing news last night."

"Oh?" Katie fiddled with a button on her dress.

"Detective Campbell spoke with Officer Bailey yesterday."

Katie glanced toward the door, as if afraid the policeman was listening to this conversation. But she quickly recovered and said innocently, "Oh? How does that affect my case?"

"What makes you think it would?"

The innocence left her. Her eyes focused, and her tone became matter-of-fact as she answered the question. "You wouldn't be telling me about it if it didn't."

He didn't have time for word duels. "That's true. Officer Bailey is going to testify that he saw you riding your bicycle back toward the Honey House from the direction of Shipwreck Point on the night of the murder."

"Perhaps he saw someone else."

Now Titus was angry. "I can't defend you if you're going to lie to me. Either tell me the truth or get yourself another lawyer."

Katie Sullivan chewed on her lip as she fought back tears. It took a minute for her to get control of herself. Once she did, she said defiantly, "All right. I wasn't in my room that evening. But I didn't kill Nate Cooper, either."

"Where were you?"

Stubbornly, Katie Sullivan shook her head. "I can't tell you. There are some clients who could make my life unbearable if it became known that they were my clients."

"But if you were with a client, he could provide you with an alibi."

"Trust me, Mr. Strong. Clients of a certain status would rather see me hang than soil their reputation."

He couldn't argue with her about that. There was no point in brow-beating the woman. But he didn't want to see her convicted of a murder she didn't commit. He'd just have to find another way.

CHAPTER 31

Titus Strong entered the Whitby District Court, Elisabeth Wade and her stenography pad following right behind him. Murder wasn't a common occurrence in the town of Whitby, certainly not one involving two residents as well-known as the lighthouse keeper and the town's most popular madam; the spectator seats in the courtroom were already beginning to fill up.

As he strode confidently down the center aisle, he caught a whiff of roses. For a moment, its familiarity interrupted his thoughts of the hearing, but he quickly banished the distraction in favor of examining his surroundings.

Smaller than the Boston courtrooms he was used to, there were only a few rows of chairs for the general public, and tables just big enough for three, maybe four, people each for the prosecution and defense. A wooden railing separated the tables from the spectators with a gate to allow people to pass from one area to the other. Titus and his secretary passed through and took seats at the left-hand table.

The judge's bench and witness chair were on a raised platform, the empty jury box on the wall to his right. He'd almost prefer the jury box were full, but it was his policy to make the judicial process as short as possible for his clients, and thus he treated the preliminary hearing as seriously as the trial.

Two men sat at the other table. From his demeanor, he assumed the one with the serious expression and large ears was Edgar Garner, the prosecutor. His naturally curly, light brown hair lay somewhat askew, despite a liberal application of pomade. His mustache was much more tidy. The second man must have been an assistant of some kind.

"I want you to take detailed notes, Miss Wade," Titus said as he stopped behind the first chair at the defense table. "You never know what piece of trivia might prove critical to a case until all the pieces of the puzzle have been laid on the table."

She nodded as she sat in the far chair, leaving the seat between them for their client. "I won't miss a word. Unless I run out of paper."

Strong quickly glanced down at the pad and verified that it was a new one with plenty of blank pages. And Miss Wade, being as efficient as any secretary he'd ever worked with, had a second pad underneath the first. When he looked up at her face, he saw her smile to let him know she was joking. He hoped she realized this was a serious situation not meant for humor.

Before he could take his seat, the prosecutor crossed the aisle and extended his right hand. "Edgar Garner. I'm so pleased to meet you, Mr. Strong."

Titus shook his hand using a carefully restrained grasp. He took note that Garner's grip was firm and dry. The man was not at all nervous about his case or the prospect of doing battle with a seasoned defense attorney. *Good!* Titus loved a fair fight. "And I, you."

"I hope being away from your home territory won't prove too much of a disadvantage." Garner's eyes had a slight twinkle as he studied Strong's face while waiting for his response.

Fortunately, a matron escorted Katie Sullivan into the courtroom, and he avoided having to make a reply either boastful or misleading. "I see my client has arrived. Perhaps we could speak some other time."

Garner turned his eyes toward Mrs. Sullivan. "Of course." He returned to his table and leaned over to whisper in his assistant's ear.

Titus pulled out Katie's chair for her. He would have done it anyway, but he wanted those present to see he was treating her like a lady, not a whore. They may not have any say in the decision made in the courtroom, but it never did any harm to influence the court of public opinion.

"I'm frightened," Mrs. Sullivan said in a soft voice.

"There's no need to be," Titus said with more confidence than he felt. "This will be over before you know it. Please sit down."

"That's what I'm afraid of." Mrs. Sullivan sat in the chair and worried her lip.

"Don't worry," Miss Wade said as she patted Mrs. Sullivan's hand. "You have the best lawyer in Whitby. I'd have to say he's the best defense attorney in Massachusetts."

Mrs. Sullivan stopped chewing her lip and smiled weakly at his secretary.

A man's voice rang out over the sound of conversation. "His honor, Judge Caleb Dewey."

An elderly man with white hair and a short beard to match came through a doorway behind and to the right of the bench. He had eyes that were sunken into his face and slanted down at the sides, lending him the appearance of someone who was past the age of hearing cases. He took his seat and spoke in a commanding voice. The minute he started, Titus changed his mind about the judge being too old for the job. "This is the preliminary hearing to determine if the accused, Mrs. Katie Sullivan, should be bound over for trial for the murder of Nate Cooper. Please accord this proceeding with the same respect as you would the trial itself." He directed the last statement toward the spectators, many of whom had continued to chat among themselves after the clerk's announcement. To drive home his point, the judge added, "If any of you are disruptive to this hearing, you will be escorted out to the street where you may continue whatever business you think is so important you can't keep quiet."

Titus held back a chuckle. He already liked this judge.

"The prosecutor may call his first witness," Judge Dewey said.

"I call Dr. Wesley Wood to the stand." Garner came out from behind the table and walked confidently toward the witness chair to wait.

A dapper man with a dark mustache rose from his seat in the first row, carefully placed the derby hat that had been in his lap on his chair, and proceeded to the witness stand. After he was sworn in, Prosecutor Garner began questioning him.

"What is your name?"

"Wesley Wood."

"And what is your title?"

"I am the Medical Examiner for the county."

"What are your qualifications?"

"I am a physician fully trained in postmortem examinations and the science of autopsy." He followed this with a list of his credentials and the number of years he'd been Medical Examiner.

"Did you examine the body of Nate Cooper?"

"I did."

"Can you tell us the state of said body regarding the cause of death?"

"The victim had been deceased for approximately eight hours. His clothing exhibited a large amount of blood from two bullet wounds, one in the shoulder and one in the chest. I confirmed the cause during the autopsy, where I extracted two bullets from the deceased."

Garner took a few steps toward the prosecutor's table, where his assistant handed him a small box. He returned to his position next to the witness, opened the box, and presented it to Dr. Wood. "Are these the two bullets you removed from Nate Cooper's body?"

The doctor peered into the box, then checked the lid. "Yes. I placed them in this box myself and marked the box before turning it over to the police."

The prosecutor addressed the judge. "I would like the bullets admitted into evidence as people's exhibit number one."

"Any objections?" the judge asked Titus Strong.

"No objections."

"The clerk of the court will label the box and the bullets Exhibit 1," the judge ordered.

Garner continued his examination of the witness. "Can you determine which one of the wounds was the cause of death?"

"The wound to the shoulder was not life-threatening, passing straight through the muscle mass. The wound to the chest pierced the sternum and struck the right ventricle of the heart, leading to massive blood loss. It was the second wound that was fatal."

"Thank you, Dr. Wood." Garner faced Titus Strong. "You may cross-examine the witness."

Titus rose from his seat and took Garner's place. "You said you examined the body eight hours after death, is that correct?"

The doctor nodded. "Yes, it is."

"Where did you perform this examination?"

"At my examining room in Brockton, Massachusetts."

"You did not examine the body at the crime scene?"

"No." For the first time, the doctor looked anxious rather than confident. "The murder was committed late at night in the middle of a ferocious storm. I wasn't made aware of the situation until the undertaker's carriage delivered Mr. Cooper to my office the next morning."

"Is that a usual circumstance in Plymouth County?"

"It is, especially when the cause of death is obvious to local police."

Things were a lot different in Boston than in Whitby. Titus would have to hope to discover something that would help his case by asking more questions. "Did you perform an autopsy?"

Wood looked affronted. "Of course I did. I'm very thorough."

"And you could determine no other possible cause of death?"

"There was none."

"Were there any medical conditions revealed by the autopsy?"

"The liver was scarred and shrunken, indicating cirrhosis."

"Will you explain the disease?"

"In cirrhosis, the liver loses function, which leads to shrinking and hardening of the organ. Most often, the cause is drinking to excess."

"What are the consequences of this loss of function?" Strong asked.

"The liver loses its ability to filter toxins from the blood. This may result in a high level of ammonia in the blood, not enough iron, and damage to blood vessels due to portal hypertension."

"Is it possible Mr. Cooper died as a result of his cirrhosis?"

"He may have died from it in time, but the immediate cause of death was definitely being shot."

Titus thought a few seconds, then said. "Thank you, doctor. I have no more questions."

CHAPTER 32

"The prosecutor may call his next witness," Judge Dewey said.

Garner rose to his feet. "I call Officer Timothy Kelley to the stand."

Tim Kelley, wearing his police uniform and blinking rapidly, was sworn in and took his seat in the witness chair. He nervously tapped his foot until the judge gave him a stern look. Titus didn't understand the anxiety. Kelley must have testified at a hearing before. *What was different about this time?*

"Officer Kelley," Garner began, "Where were you on the night of July second?"

"I was on the evening shift. There was a violent thunderstorm raging that night, and I was trying to keep as dry as I could. I didn't roam far from the police station because of the weather. Usually, we have only one officer on duty, but Chief Morgan thought there might be need of more manpower because of the storm."

"Did anything unusual happen that night?"

"Mostly, it was quiet. People didn't want to be out, you know. But I heard the cannon fire, and ran toward the beach, knowing what to expect. A schooner had wrecked on the sandbar off Whitby Beach."

"You heard a cannon fire?"

"Yes, sir. I knew it was the cannon they use to send a line out for the breeches buoy. To rescue survivors still on the ship."

"And you ran for the beach then?"

"I did. I knew they'd need plenty of help if the wreck was bad."

"What did you see when you got to the beach?"

"When the lightning flashed, I could see the spars and lines of a ship. From the way they were tilted, I knew she'd run aground on the sandbar. The lifesaving crew seemed to have things under control, but I stuck around in case I was needed."

"What happened next?"

"I encountered Mr. Strong on the beach. I saw him dive into the water and help a man to shore."

"You ran into the defense attorney?" Garner sounded incredulous, but Titus knew it was an act. No smart attorney asked a question he didn't know the answer to. Garner was definitely smart.

"Yes, sir. I imagine, like anyone, he'd come out to see what was going on. Then, when he saw the poor man struggling, he went in to help him."

"Please don't tell us what you imagined, Officer Kelley. Please stick to the facts."

Titus suppressed a grin. The testimony of his heroism had

already been written into the record. Garner was doing his job for him.

"Sorry, sir."

"Did you speak to Mr. Strong?"

"Yes, I did. I congratulated him on his effort, and we got to talking. He asked if it were common to have shipwrecks now that there was a lighthouse. That caused the two of us to look toward the Point. We saw that there was no light coming from the lighthouse, which explained why the ship hadn't known to go around."

"What did you do then?"

"I ran down to the Point to find out why the light was out. I didn't want another ship to wreck in the storm."

"Did Mr. Strong accompany you?"

"He did. But I made sure I entered the keeper's cottage first. If there was something amiss, I didn't want a civilian tampering with any possible evidence."

"So even before entering the lighthouse, you thought a crime might have been committed?"

"It was possible. It was Nate Cooper's job to keep the light in proper working order and lit during the night. It crossed my mind that something might have prevented him from performing his duty."

Several of the spectators tittered at that statement. Even before the M.E.'s testimony, most of the population of Whitby must have been aware of Cooper's drinking problem.

"What did you find when you entered the cottage?"

"The cottage was a mess. Not that Nate kept it neat when he lived there, but I think he usually closed the desk drawers. Once I got over the mess, I saw poor Nate on the floor, shot."

"Was he alive when you saw him?"

"No, sir. He wasn't breathing and there was an awful lot of blood."

"Where was this blood?"

"Most of it was soaking his shirt near the middle of his chest. Some was dripping onto the carpet."

"Was Mr. Cooper bleeding from another wound?"

"He was. There was a smaller spot of blood on his shoulder."

"Did you examine the wounds?"

"Examine?"

"Did you look for where the blood was coming from?"

"I knew where it was coming from."

"Please explain how you knew where it was coming from."

"There was a derringer on the floor beside the body. It didn't take much to know that he'd been shot with it."

The prosecutor retrieved an item with a tag hanging from it from his table. "Is this the derringer you saw next to Nate Cooper's body?"

"Yes. It's a very distinctive weapon with the engraving on the nickel coating and the pearl handle. I put that tag on it myself."

"I'd like the derringer admitted as people's exhibit number two."

"No objection," Strong said.

Garner handed the derringer to the court clerk. "What did you do then?"

"I told Mr. Strong to watch the door and keep others out while I searched the premises. I determined that no one else was in the cottage or the lighthouse at that time."

"Let's go back to July first, the day before the shipwreck. Did you have occasion to be called to the Seaview Hotel?"

"I did. There was a report of a loud argument on the second floor. Since, as I said, I was on the evening shift that week, I went to the hotel to investigate."

"And what did you find when you arrived?"

"Mrs. Sullivan was shouting at Nate Cooper. She had a derringer pointed at him."

"Was this the derringer she was using?" Garner pointed to the gun that had been admitted into evidence.

"I can't say for sure. A derringer is so small, you can't see much of it when it's in someone's hand. I do remember the light glinting off the barrel, so it was shiny like this one."

"What was the subject of the argument?"

"Well, Nate, I mean Mr. Cooper, was holding onto the sleeve of one of Mrs. Sullivan's girls. Her dress was ripped, showing that there'd been a struggle."

"What did Mrs. Sullivan say?"

"She told Mr. Cooper to let go of Emily—that's the name of the girl he was holding."

"And did he?"

"Not right away. Chief Morgan had to talk to him before he let go."

"Did Mrs. Sullivan sound angry to you?"

"Yes, sir. She was shouting, and her face was all scrunched up, if you know what I mean."

"Indeed, I do. Did she sound angry enough to shoot Nate Cooper?"

"Objection!" Strong roared as he rose to his feet. "Calls for a conclusion on the part of the witness."

"Sustained," Judge Dewey said with a shake of his head.

Garner continued, unperturbed. "Was the situation resolved satisfactorily?"

"I'm not sure what you mean, Mr. Garner. Mr. Cooper let go of Emily. The argument was over as far as I could tell. The chief and I went back to the station then."

"I have no more questions, your honor."

Judge Dewey looked down at his watch. "Seeing as it's almost noon, we will adjourn for lunch. You may cross-examine this witness when we resume at two o'clock, Mr. Strong."

CHAPTER 33

ELISABETH WAS SURPRISED when Titus Strong asked her if she wanted to go to lunch with him. She wasn't certain lunching with your boss was appropriate behavior. You had to be so careful of your reputation, particularly in a town like Whitby where women were divided into two types: the good women and the bad. "I was planning on typing up this morning's notes so you'd have them available to you for your cross-examination."

"I took enough notes on things I want to bring out from Tim Kelley." He showed her his notepad, which had writing on only the top third. When he saw her looking askance at him, he added, "Besides, if I need more information, I can always ask you to translate your Pitman for me."

Elisabeth hesitated. It would be pleasant to have a nice lunch for a change. She didn't cook much since her father had passed away and usually brought lunch in a paper sack to save money.

"Oh, Elisabeth," Amanda Cooper sang from nearby.

Startled, she observed her former classmate. Amanda was appropriately dressed in black, with a heavy veil over her features. "Hello, Amanda. Mr. Strong, this is Amanda Cooper, Nate Cooper's daughter. We went to school together. Amanda, Titus Strong."

"I'm pleased to meet you, Miss Cooper, and I'm sorry for your loss."

"I'm surprised to see you at this hearing," Elisabeth said. "I would think it would be too painful to hear all the testimony about your father."

"It is, some," Amanda said. "But you have to realize that I hadn't seen my father in years, so it's not as painful as it might otherwise be."

"We were just going to have lunch," Strong said. "Would you care to join us?"

"Oh, no." Amanda sounded flustered. "I can't be seen in a public restaurant while I'm in mourning. It wouldn't be appropriate. But I did want to thank you for rescuing me the night of the storm."

Elisabeth's head swiveled in Mr. Strong's direction. He hadn't said anything to her about rescuing the man that Tim Kelley had testified about. Now it turned out he'd rescued Amanda, too?

Titus Strong seemed as confused as Elisabeth felt. "I didn't rescue you."

"Oh, but you did. I'd gotten all turned around while I was swimming from the schooner. If I hadn't heard you shouting at me to turn toward shore, I probably would have been pulled out to sea. I looked for you once I reached land, but you weren't there." Amanda paused a moment.

And neither were you, if what you told me last week was true. Elisabeth wished she could catch Amanda's eye, but Amanda studiously kept her gaze focused on Mr. Strong.

"I guess that's when you and Officer Kelley went to the lighthouse."

"It must have been," Strong said. "I hate to cut you short, Miss Cooper, but Miss Wade and I need to eat lunch and prepare for the afternoon session."

"Oh, of course. I don't want to hold you up." Amanda shifted her attention from Strong to Elisabeth. "We'll have to talk again sometime."

"Yes, we will." *About several things.* She watched Amanda's back as she walked away.

"Shall we go to the pub?"

Elisabeth had almost forgotten her boss was standing there. "Would it be an appropriate place for a lady?"

"It would, as long as you're accompanied by a gentleman." His smile was so warm she blushed in response.

"Officer Kelley," Titus began at the start of the afternoon session. "You testified that you thought something might be amiss when the lighthouse was dark on the night of the storm. Did you assume someone had incapacitated Mr. Cooper before we reached the keeper's cottage?"

Tim Kelley's face reddened. "No."

"What did you think might be the situation?"

"Well, sir, Nate Cooper was known to take a drink or two."

Again, the spectators chuckled.

"Did he sometimes have more than two drinks?"

"Yes, sir."

"More than three?"

Tim Kelley nodded. "Old Nate could drink a lot. I thought most likely he'd passed out from drinking before he could light the lamp." The officer looked chagrined. "It wouldn't be the first time."

"Had he been drinking on the night he had the argument with Mrs. Sullivan?"

"I'd say so."

"Why would you 'say so'?"

"Nate was none too steady on his feet, and his speech was slurred."

"Could you smell liquor on his breath?"

"I didn't get close enough to him for that."

"In your experience as a police officer, is someone more likely to get belligerent when they've had a drink or two?"

"I object!" Garner shouted. "The witness is not an expert on psychology."

"Let me rephrase the question," Strong said. "In your experience with the victim, was he more likely to get belligerent after a few drinks than when he was sober?"

"That's for sure. I'd had to break up several fights Mr. Cooper started when he was drinking."

"Let me direct your attention to the murder weapon. You stated that you couldn't say if the derringer that killed Nate Cooper was the same as Mrs. Sullivan used during her argument with him at the hotel."

"That's right."

"You also said that you saw the light glint off the barrel."

"I did."

"When you noticed the barrel at the Seaview Hotel, could you see the distinctive scrollwork that this derringer has?"

"No, sir. I wasn't close enough to see anything like that."

"Did you see any part of the pearl handle on that night?"

"Like I said, Mr. Strong, the grip was covered by Mrs. Sullivan's hand."

"So Mrs. Sullivan could have been holding an entirely different derringer that night?"

"Yes, sir."

Titus thought he'd gotten as much from the police officer as he could at this time. He'd made Nate Cooper out to be an ornery drunk and cast doubt on the connection between Katie Sullivan and the murder weapon. He'd have to hope future witnesses would strengthen his case. "No further questions."

CHAPTER 34

As soon as Tim Kelley had taken his seat, the prosecutor called out, "I call Miss Amanda Cooper to the stand."

Elisabeth's heart skipped a beat. *What could Amanda be testifying to?* She watched as her old friend walked slowly to the front of the courtroom and was sworn in. With the veil covering her face, it was impossible to read her expression. Elisabeth wondered what she was feeling. She almost forgot to take down what was said, but recovered in time to catch up.

"First of all," the prosecutor said, "I know I speak for everyone in this courtroom when I say I am sorry that your father died in such a horrible way."

"Thank you, Mr. Garner." Her voice was slightly muffled behind the nearly opaque veil. "I'm willing to help in any way I can to see that justice is done."

"I believe you and your mother left Whitby a number of years ago. Is that right?"

"That's true. My mother had the delicate nature of a southern gentlewoman. The harsh winters and the fact that my father worked nights were too much for her to bear. About five years ago, she knew she had to return to Richmond, Virginia or perish. I went with her."

That wasn't the woman Elisabeth remembered. Oh, Mrs. Cooper had fanned herself rapidly in the summer, and often got "the vapors" when things weren't going her way. But beneath that fragile exterior, the woman had a core of iron.

"What brought you back to Whitby at this point in time?"

"Unfortunately, the gentle southern climate wasn't enough to cure her. Or maybe we had gone to Richmond too late. My dear mother passed away last month. Once everything was settled, I thought it was time to visit my father after all those years."

Amanda was playing the role of a southern belle to the hilt.

"How did you travel?"

"I took a schooner north. I thought it would be the easiest way. But then we got caught in that terrible storm…" Amanda's voice broke.

Garner handed her a handkerchief from his breast pocket. "I'm so sorry. Take your time, Miss Cooper."

The woman dabbed at her eyes and nose under the veil. At least, that's what Elisabeth assumed she was doing from the sniffs and the little lumps that appeared on the surface of the fabric as her hand moved beneath it.

"I'm ready now."

"You were saying the schooner you were sailing on was caught in the storm."

"It was. We were tossed around in our bunks like so many

corks bouncing on the waves. The rain blew under the doors and I thought the wind would tear the ship apart. And then there was a horrific thud, and the ship tilted sideways. That must have been when it ran aground on the sandbar.

"The ship's crew was yelling at us to get off the ship. One said it was going to sink. People were leaping over the side, and I thought I'd better do that, too.

"The water was so rough, I had trouble keeping afloat."

Elisabeth's pencil scritched across the page as the pressure from her hand broke the point. Mr. Strong was looking at her curiously, so she quickly picked up her spare pencil and mouthed "Sorry" at him.

Amanda Cooper was a strong swimmer. No matter how rough the water, Elisabeth couldn't imagine her having trouble keeping afloat.

"There were so many people in the water. Everyone was crying and screaming, and then there was that big boom. I was so frightened, I thought my heart would stop beating. In the confusion, I got all turned around. I didn't know which way the shore was. Fortunately, there was a man yelling at me, and a boat drew up next to me. The men in the boat pulled me in. They saved me from drowning."

"That must have been a terrible ordeal for you."

"Oh, it was. I'm not sure I've recovered from it yet."

"When did you learn your father had been murdered?"

"The next day. I was taken to a boarding house where I dried off and got into bed. The next morning, when I went down to breakfast, there was an extra edition of the newspaper. There was a sketch of the shipwreck, but the headline said Lighthouse Keeper Murdered. I couldn't believe it meant my father. Surely he had taken some other job since my dear mother and I left Whitby. But it was." She was sobbing again. "I couldn't believe it, losing a mother and a father in the same summer. Now I have no one." Amanda's head fell on her chest as she wailed the last words.

Elisabeth took the opportunity to lean close to Mr. Strong and whisper, "I have to talk to you before you cross-examine her."

He looked surprised for a minute, but then nodded that he understood.

"Your honor," the prosecutor said. "Obviously, Miss Cooper is too prostrate with grief and the memory of her ordeal to continue today. I have no more questions for her at this time, and I would request a short recess before Mr. Strong conducts his cross-examination."

"Mr. Strong, do you have any objections?" Judge Dewey asked.

Strong rose to his feet. "No, your honor. In fact, I have no questions for this witness at this time. But I reserve my right to cross-examine Miss Cooper at a future time."

"Granted." The judge addressed the courtroom at large. "Due to the lateness of the hour, we shall adjourn until ten o'clock tomorrow morning."

Elisabeth closed her stenographer's pad and picked up her pencils. Strong had remained standing, so she got to her feet. Meanwhile, everyone else had started leaving. The spectators filled the room with chatter, most likely about Amanda's testimony. There was nothing of more interest than local gossip about a hometown girl.

"What did you want to talk to me about?" Mr. Strong asked

her as he joined the throng leaving the courtroom.

"I'd prefer to wait until we're back at the office."

"Let's hurry, then."

Titus sat at his desk and glanced at the small pot-bellied stove.

"Would you like some coffee?"

Elisabeth Wade almost seemed to read his mind. He couldn't have found a better secretary. Not even in Boston. "That would be wonderful, Miss Wade." He hesitated, wondering if what he was about to do would be considered too forward. He decided if it was, he'd just have to apologize. "Miss Wade seems so formal. We'll be working a lot of hours together. Would you mind if I called you Elisabeth?"

Her smile was warm when she replied. "Not at all."

He couldn't help but smile back at her. "Elisabeth, then. And you must call me Titus."

She looked doubtful for a minute, then nodded.

"Now, how about that coffee, Elisabeth?"

"I'll get it started right away, Titus." She hesitated a little before saying his name. At the end of it, she worked her mouth, as if figuring out how it tasted on her tongue. Then, seeming satisfied with the flavor of it, she busied herself with filling the coffeepot with water and ground coffee.

Meanwhile, Titus tried to decipher his handwritten notes from today's testimony. The Medical Examiner had established the cause of death. Officer Kelley had served to describe the crime scene and the argument at the hotel the night before. He'd been surprised at the "testimony" from Amanda Cooper. Usually, the tactic of building sympathy toward the victim in order to make the accused appear more guilty was reserved for the trial, where there was a jury it could influence. He wondered if that was what Elisabeth wanted to discuss.

The aroma of freshly brewed coffee filled his office, and moments later Elisabeth set a cup in front of him. She'd also poured a cup for herself. "I thought you only drank tea," he said with a smile.

"Usually, but I've gotten so used to making coffee for you and taking a cup for myself, I've grown to enjoy it more than I ever thought I would." She took a sip.

Titus did the same. "Now, what was so important that you had to whisper about it during the hearing?"

"I've known Amanda Cooper most of my life. We were particularly friendly in our early years, and we still got together during the summers after we graduated from eighth grade. During the winter, we didn't see much of one another. My parents insisted I attend high school, even though I had no intention of going to college, while Amanda's mother was more interested in ensuring she became a proper lady and meet a marriageable young man."

Having a high school education was unusual for a woman, although it was becoming more common now. No wonder Elisabeth was such an exemplary secretary.

She paused to take another sip of coffee, then put her cup on his desk, being careful to place it on top of the blotter so it wouldn't leave a ring. "Like most residents of Whitby, Amanda is—or was—a very strong swimmer. In fact, she often won competitions among us girls. So I can't imagine her losing her head and getting turned around even during a storm such as we had."

"The water was very rough. I'm a strong swimmer myself,

and it took all my effort to bring that man to shore." He hesitated, not wanting to admit any weakness to Elisabeth, but in the end decided honesty was best. "In fact, I was extremely grateful when Miss Cooper got close enough to the rowboat for them to pull her in. I wasn't sure I had enough strength left to go in a second time."

For a moment, Elisabeth seemed taken aback, but she quickly regained her composure. "That's not the only thing she said that didn't make sense."

"Oh?"

"On my first day working for you, I ran into Amanda in town. She was the old friend I mentioned. She was buying mourning clothes." Elisabeth paused, as if there were some significance to that fact.

"Isn't that usual when a family member dies?"

"Yes. But if her mother had died only a few months before she came to Whitby, she should have brought a whole wardrobe of mourning clothes with her. Why would she need to buy them after she got here?"

Titus picked up his pen and started tapping it on his desk while he thought. "I don't know too much about women's mourning clothes. It's much easier for a man, I imagine. A black suit and, later, a black armband are all men have to worry about wearing."

"But there's a whole ritual of mourning for women. For one thing, as she said when you asked her to lunch, going out wouldn't be at all appropriate."

"Wait a minute. Amanda Cooper wouldn't have had any clothes she brought with her. They would have been lost, or at least ruined, when the schooner wrecked in the storm. So it makes perfect sense that she had to buy new mourning clothes after she arrived in Whitby."

"Well, that's another thing." Elisabeth leaned forward. "On that first day, she told me she'd come to Whitby as soon as she heard about her father's death. She said she'd taken the train up the coast. She didn't say anything about being on the schooner."

Since Titus himself had aided Amanda Cooper's rescue the night of the storm, it didn't seem likely she'd not been in Whitby until several days later. "Isn't it possible you misunderstood her? Or that in her grief, she had gotten confused?"

For a moment, Elisabeth looked as if she were going to argue with him. Then she appeared to change her mind. "It's possible," she said slowly. "Why don't I try to talk to her alone tomorrow and make sure what I heard is what she said."

"That sounds like a good idea." Titus stifled a yawn, then grinned guiltily in his secretary's direction. "I apologize. It's been a long day, and I have a feeling tomorrow will be longer. Let me get you a hansom cab since the trolley has stopped running by now, and we'll talk again in the morning."

"There's no need to get me a cab. As always, I rode my bicycle into town."

"Will it be safe to ride home? It's starting to get dark. You could lock your bicycle in my office and take the trolley in the morning."

Elisabeth set her shoulders, and her face became stern. "I'll be perfectly fine on my bicycle."

Stubborn woman. He wasn't sure if that made her less attractive. Or more.

CHAPTER 35

Upon entering the courtroom the next morning, the first thing Elisabeth Wade did was look for Amanda Cooper. She'd hoped to arrange either lunch or dinner right away, but it looked as if she'd have to wait. Amanda hadn't come to the hearing this morning.

Elisabeth wished she'd asked her where she was staying yesterday, but she hadn't, and so didn't know where to find her childhood friend. She wondered if Mr. Strong would agree to have Owen Campbell track her down if she didn't show up at the hearing again. As the judge gaveled the proceedings to order, she had to postpone thinking about Amanda and concentrate on the next witness. She opened her stenographer's pad to the first blank page and picked up her newly sharpened pencil.

"I call Tom Hinkle to the witness stand," Edgar Garner announced after the preliminaries were taken care of. Once

Hinkle was sworn in, he began his interrogation.

"Were you at the Seaview Hotel on the night of July first?"

Elisabeth thought she heard a soft whimper beside her. She flicked a glance in their client's direction. Mrs. Sullivan was pressing her lips together. She looked worried.

"I was there." Hinkle looked uncomfortable in a newly purchased suit and his slicked back hair.

"Tell us what happened that evening?"

"I was playing poker in Golden Chances."

"After you played poker, then what did you do?"

"Well, I drank at the bar for a while." His lips formed an embarrassed grin. "Had a few too many, and I decided to stay the night at the hotel rather than going back to my place."

"What room did you stay in?"

"Two-oh-seven, I think it was. It could have been 209. I remember it was on the second floor."

"Did you go right to sleep?"

"It didn't take me long, as I remember."

"Did anything wake you up in the middle of the night?"

"It sure did. There was a big ruckus in the hall. Two people yelling at one another, a man and a woman. I opened my door to see what was going on."

"What did you see?"

"I saw Mrs. Sullivan there," he looked toward the defendant, "and she was mighty angry with Nate Cooper. He was holding on to Emily as tightly as a Gloucester man hangs onto a swordfish once it's landed on the deck. Emily was squirming like a fish, too."

The courtroom erupted in laughter.

"Order in the court," the judge demanded as he pounded his

gavel. "If the spectators can't restrain themselves, I'll have to clear the courtroom."

The judge's scowl was enough to suppress further outbursts from the crowd.

"What were they arguing about?"

Hinkle's face reddened. "I don't like to say with ladies present."

"Would the judge instruct the witness to answer the question?" Garner said.

"The witness will respond to the question. If any ladies are offended, they are free to leave the courtroom."

Elisabeth fought back a smile. She couldn't imagine any of the ladies of Whitby—proper or otherwise—wanting to miss the most salacious part of the testimony.

"Well, it sounded like Nate wanted Emily's... um... favors without paying for them. Seeing as how Mrs. Sullivan makes her living from her girls selling those favors, she wasn't real happy about the situation."

"Was she more than unhappy?"

"I'll say she was. She was spittin' mad."

A titter started up again, but abruptly cut off when the judge frowned at the offenders.

"Was Mrs. Sullivan doing more than shouting at Nate Cooper?"

"She sure was. She was pointing a gun at him."

"Did you get a good look at that gun?" Garner asked.

"Well, not right away, but later on the police showed up, and when the chief started talking, she dropped it."

"She dropped the gun?"

"Uh huh. I mean, yes, she did."

"Did you get a good look at the gun then?"

"I sure did. I remember it was really fancy, a real lady's gun."

Garner brought the derringer that had been admitted as evidence over to Hinkle on the witness stand. "Is this the gun Mrs. Sullivan pointed at Nate Cooper?"

"That's it!" Hinkle said excitedly.

"Are you sure this is the gun Mrs. Sullivan threatened Nate Cooper with?"

"Of course I'm sure."

"No further questions." Garner gave Titus Strong a smug look.

Elisabeth watched as Titus rose to his feet. He had a trim physique, and there was a sense of being in total control about him. When he spoke, he spoke with authority.

"Mr. Hinkle."

Tom Hinkle straightened in his chair at the sound of the defense attorney's voice.

Mr. Strong picked up the derringer and showed it to the witness. "You're sure this is the weapon you saw in Katie Sullivan's hand the night of the argument at the Seaview Hotel?"

"I'm sure."

Did he look apprehensive?

"You've testified that Mrs. Sullivan dropped the weapon when confronted by the chief of police."

"Yes."

"Did you see Mrs. Sullivan pick up the derringer after it fell to the floor?"

Hinkle shook his head. "No, sir. I mean, I'm not sure."

"You're not sure whether she picked it up or you're not sure if you saw her pick it up?"

"I don't remember." He forced his mouth to form a smile. "I don't remember seeing Mrs. Sullivan pick it up."

"Do you remember anyone else picking up the derringer?"

"I don't. After all the fireworks were over, I went back in my room."

"So, as far as you know, anyone could have picked up the derringer after Mrs. Sullivan dropped it."

"There weren't that many people there."

"But any one of them could have taken the derringer after the others had returned to their rooms?"

"I guess so."

"Where are you employed?" Strong asked.

Hinkle started, as if this were the last question he expected anyone to ask him. Elisabeth wondered why. It was an innocuous question.

"I work at the Payne Salvage Yard."

"And how long have you been employed there?"

"Five or six years."

"Would you say you have a good working relationship with your employer?"

Hinkle squirmed. "Mr. Payne? He's all right. He doesn't spend much time at the yard."

"Are you given fair recompense for your labors?"

"Huh?"

"Do you feel you are paid fairly for the work you do at the salvage yard?"

Hinkle ran a finger around inside his collar. Elisabeth wondered if the starched fabric was irritating his neck.

"I guess I am."

"Do you sometimes do other work to increase your income?"

"Like what?"

"Oh, I don't know. But seeing this is Whitby, might you sometimes hire on with a fishing boat?"

"No, sir. I don't do anything like that."

"And no work other than at the salvage yard."

"No, sir." His upper lip glistened.

"I have no further questions at this time," Mr. Strong said.

CHAPTER 36

As he and Miss Wade walked to the pub for lunch, Titus could see by the look on her face she was deliberating over something. "What is it, Elisabeth?"

"I've been watching how you cross-examine witnesses."

Titus chuckled. "I hope so. I'm counting on your notes to refer to as I build my defense strategy."

She smiled up at him. "Oh, I've been taking thorough notes as well. But I noticed you treated Hinkle differently than the other witnesses."

"How so?"

"Well, the beginning was okay. You questioned him on the derringer, and then made the point that he didn't know Katie Sullivan had the gun after the argument at the hotel. That was to plant doubt that she actually had the gun to shoot Nate Cooper with."

She was sharp. Perhaps she was sharper than he'd given her credit for.

"But?"

"What was all of that about Hinkle working at the salvage yard and asking him if he took on other jobs?"

"You remember Owen Campbell found out Hinkle was stealing from the salvage yard? I didn't want to challenge him with that yet, but I wanted to open the door to the possibility of asking him about it later. A hearing is like a game of chess. You have to get your pieces in the right positions to set up an attack. I was maneuvering Hinkle into a spot where I might be able to convince the judge that he is as likely a suspect as Katie Sullivan."

Miss Wade was quiet for a while. Then she said, "A courtroom is a fascinating place."

"It definitely is," Titus agreed.

The hearing resumed promptly at 2:00 PM.

"I call Officer Barney Bailey to the stand," Edgar Garner announced.

The aging, rotund police officer walked up the aisle to the witness box and was sworn in. He removed his helmet and held it in his lap after he sat down.

"Officer Bailey, will you please tell the court what you were doing on the night of July second of this year."

Bailey cleared his throat with a harrumph. "I was patrolling, like I always do when I'm on shift." He gave a superior look to Tim Kelley, as if to say you might stay in the office when you're on the night shift, but I'm out and about no matter what time it is or what the weather. "I'd rode my bicycle down to the cottages just south of Shipwreck Point. I do that often at night, since the rich have more worth stealing than the poor."

A few of the spectators laughed, but quickly stopped when Judge Dewey pounded his gavel.

"At what time were you near the cottages?"

"I was there twice that night. I went down once at about 8:00 PM and again around midnight."

"What was the weather like that night?"

"It weren't too bad early in the evening. The wind was picking up a bit, and there was a little bit of rain. Later on, though... Whee-oh! That wind was howling, the rain was coming down in buckets, and I never saw so much lightning."

"Did you see anything of note while on your patrol of Whitby?"

"Not at eight o'clock. Monday nights are generally quiet, what with people having to work the next day."

Garner took a deep breath and let it out slowly. "Did you see anything on the second circuit of the town?"

Bailey nodded his head vigorously. "Indeed, I did, sir. I saw her"—he pointed to Katie Sullivan—"riding her bicycle full speed ahead away from the Point."

"Did you speak with Mrs. Sullivan?"

"No, sir. She didn't look like she wanted to be talked to."

"Can you elaborate?"

"Well, she was starin' straight ahead like she couldn't even see me. Her hands were wrapped around the grips of her handlebars like she wanted to choke the life out of them. If they were alive, I mean."

Someone giggled, but cut the laugh off as if suddenly remembering the judge's warning.

"You said she was riding her bicycle away from the Point."

"I did."

The Case of the Mysterious Madam

"Did you get the impression that's where she was coming from?"

"Objection!" Strong said. "Calls for a conclusion on the part of the witness."

"Agreed, Mr. Strong," the judge said. "The objection is sustained. The witness will testify as to what he knows from his own observations, not from his 'impressions'."

Garner looked put out, as if he was used to playing fast and loose with the rules of evidence. "No further questions." He looked at Titus, signifying it was the defense attorney's turn.

"Officer Bailey," Titus began. "How did you know what time it was when you saw Mrs. Sullivan on her bicycle?"

"I looked up at the clock tower on top of Town Hall when I left the police station. I remember it being 11:30 because I knew I'd have to write it down in the shift log. It takes about twenty, thirty minutes to ride out to the Point, maybe a little longer that night because of the weather. So it had to be around midnight when I saw Mrs. Sullivan."

"Did you speak to Mrs. Sullivan?"

"No, sir. Like I said, she didn't seem to be in a mood for speaking to anyone."

"Did you see her leave any particular location?"

"No."

"So you don't know whether she started her ride out at the lighthouse or at a cottage a block away."

"I can't say as I do. But I doubt she'd be at a nearby cottage. It wouldn't be respectable."

"Are you sure none of the residents of the cottages use Mrs. Sullivan's services?"

Bailey's cheeks turned red.

"Well, Officer Bailey? Are you sure none of the residents of the cottages use Mrs. Sullivan's services?"

"I couldn't be sure of that," he croaked.

"No further questions."

Titus, confident he'd discredited the implication Garner had tried to introduce by having Officer Bailey testify, returned to his seat. But Garner had one more trick up his sleeve.

"I call Fred Stevens to the stand."

Titus started to raise an objection. Stevens was on his witness list, not the prosecution's. Then he thought better of objecting. He could bring out the points he wished to make just as well on cross-examination as direct.

"Where were you on the night of July second?" Garner asked once Stevens was sworn in.

"I was staying at the Seaview Hotel."

"What floor was your room on?"

"The second floor."

"Did you witness the argument between Mrs. Sullivan and Nate Cooper?"

"Yes, I did. Like everybody else, I went out in the hall when I heard them yelling at one another."

"Did you go back into your room once Chief Morgan broke up the confrontation?"

"Not right away. The chief didn't really break it up."

"Please explain that statement."

"Well, Mrs. Sullivan wasn't pointing her derringer at old Nate anymore, but they were still having words."

"What kind of words?"

Stevens glanced at Katie Sullivan. He licked his lips. "Mrs. Sullivan said, 'You're going to pay for what you did, and I don't mean the pittance you'll come up with to give Emily.'"

"Were those her exact words? You're going to pay for what you did?" Garner asked.

"Yes, sir."

"No further questions." Again, Garner looked smugly at Titus Strong.

"I believe we've reached a good point to adjourn for the day," Judge Dewey said.

Titus didn't want the last thing the judge—or the spectators—remembered to be Katie Sullivan's threat to Nate Cooper. "Your honor, there's plenty of time left this afternoon."

"Unfortunately, I have an appointment that I must go to," the judge said. "The hearing is adjourned until ten o'clock tomorrow morning."

CHAPTER 37

ELISABETH DISMOUNTED FROM her bicycle and walked it around to the back entrance of her house. It felt strange to be arriving home so early, but Mr. Strong had told her she might leave once her stenographer's notes were typed up. As she opened the door, she was greeted by Daisy's joyful barking. The border terrier hadn't adjusted well to her new work schedule, and Elisabeth felt a twinge of guilt at leaving her alone all day. But she had to earn a living. There wasn't enough money from the sale of her father's barbershop to pay expenses after putting something toward all the medical bills from his breathing problems.

"I'll take you out in just a minute, Daisy." She wheeled her bicycle back to the woodshed and leaned it against the wall. The room had little wood in it this time of year, just enough to feed the stove in the kitchen for cooking.

The dog ran out ahead of her when she opened the entry

door and quickly fetched her favorite rubber ball. The terrier ran back and offered it to her mistress.

"All right." Elisabeth laughed as she eased the ball out of Daisy's mouth. "Here you go." She threw the ball to the back corner of the yard, avoiding the kitchen garden where she grew herbs and vegetables. The weeds had started to take over, and she made a mental note that she'd have to weed it on Saturday. After about fifteen minutes of playing fetch, the dog lay down at her feet and put her head on her paws.

"Time to go inside. We'll take our usual walk after I have supper."

She emptied the drip pan under the icebox before opening the cabinet door. It was too hot to cook, but she had some leftover mutton that could be served cold. Along with some bread and butter, it would make a nice supper. She was just about to sit at the small kitchen table when she heard a knock on the front door. She wondered if it might be one of the neighbor ladies with a casserole. After her father had passed away, there had been a seemingly endless supply of casseroles and hot dishes. This had tapered off over time, but it still wasn't unusual for one to appear now and then.

"Hello!" she heard from the other side of the door, and she picked up her pace to find out what was so urgent.

When she opened the door, she found a young woman in a somewhat shabby day dress standing on her porch. "Can I help you?"

"I'm Emily Hartwell." The girl stopped and the look on her face said she felt too intimidated to say more.

Meanwhile, Elisabeth was trying to place where she'd heard the name Emily. Then she remembered and her eyes opened wide. "Emily. You're... acquainted with... Mrs. Sullivan, is that right?"

Emily glanced to both sides to make sure no one was watching her, then nodded. "Yes. Might I come in? I don't think your neighbors would approve of someone like me visiting you."

The girl had a point. Elisabeth wondered if even now one of them was spying from behind lace curtains and taking note of her visitor. But Elisabeth couldn't leave the girl standing on the porch, gossip or no gossip. "Of course."

She stepped inside, and Elisabeth led the way to the parlor. She gestured toward the settee. "Have a seat, Emily."

Emily gawked at the furnishings. She seemed particularly taken by the clock on the mantle, an heirloom that had been passed down for several generations. "Is all this yours?"

Elisabeth looked at the familiar surroundings. She'd lived in this house all her life, and nothing had changed much over almost three decades. The wallpaper, a muted pale green with ivory stems and leaves in curlicues, had faded over time. That didn't matter much, as most of it was covered with family photos, small paintings, some of which she'd done herself, and stitchery projects made by the women who had lived in the house.

"It is now," she said, her heart heavy with the memory of her father's passing. Wanting to avoid those memories, she got down to business. "What brings you to see me this evening?"

The girl nervously raised a hand toward her mouth, then quickly put her hands in her lap. Elisabeth stole a glance at them. Her fingernails were bitten down almost to the quick, and her cuticles were ragged. "I was wondering if you knew why Mr. Strong isn't calling me as a witness."

"I think you'd have to ask him that."

"Oh, I couldn't do that! He's such an important man and all. I was hoping you knew." She looked disappointed.

Actually, she did know. "It's strange that none of the other girls at Mrs. Sullivan's saw her that evening. Only you."

"He thinks I lied."

Although that was true, Elisabeth was hesitant to say so. "Did you?"

She started to shake her head, then nodded. Her eyes glistened with tears, and she quickly raised a hand to brush them away.

Elisabeth pulled a handkerchief from her pocket and handed it to Emily.

After the girl—she really was more of a girl than a young woman—blotted her eyes, she said, "I didn't want to lie, but I know Mrs. Sullivan didn't kill that man. She couldn't have."

"I know you must be very fond of Mrs. Sullivan—"

"That's not it," Emily interrupted. "I mean, I am fond of her, but that's not the reason I know she didn't kill Mr. Cooper."

"And what is that reason?" Elisabeth asked gently.

Emily's eyes darted around the room, lit on a picture on the opposite wall. She got up and went over to where she could look at it more closely. "Are these your parents?"

"They are." She had to find some way of getting Emily to say what she'd come here to tell her. "It's all right, Emily. You can tell me whatever it is you're hiding. I won't tell anyone else unless you agree that I should."

The girl came back and sank into the place where she'd been

sitting before. In a voice as soft as a whisper, she said, "Mrs. Sullivan wasn't at the Honey House that night. She'd gone out to help a woman who needed her."

"A woman?" Elisabeth couldn't imagine any women needing the services of Katie Sullivan.

Emily again avoided looking at her, but this time she stayed seated. "Sometimes a woman gets into trouble. It happened to one of the girls at the Honey House last year. She forgot to take measures"—Emily flicked a glance in Elisabeth's direction, then quickly resumed studying the carpet—"and found herself in the family way."

Elisabeth felt a flush rise in her cheeks. She thought she had been doing so well, remaining so calm, when talking with the young prostitute. But Emily had ventured into territory Elisabeth hadn't discussed with anyone since her father had an aunt talk to her about women's monthly cycles when she was a girl.

Emily took a deep breath and raised her eyes to meet Elisabeth's. "Mrs. Sullivan knows how to stop women from having a baby. She was helping one of the women who lives in a great cottage in the rich part of Whitby."

"I assume the woman's husband would know nothing about this."

"Oh, no. It's not something you discuss with a man you're married to. If he found out, he'd be furious."

As Elisabeth could well imagine. "Would this woman be willing to testify in court?" she asked, knowing the answer before she asked the question.

"She couldn't. If she talked about it in public, there'd be such a scandal, she'd never be accepted in society again. Her husband would be shamed as well."

"Why did you tell me this, if you knew that it couldn't prove Mrs. Sullivan is innocent?"

"I was hoping you'd know some way to tell Mr. Strong, and he could figure out how to use the information to help her."

"I don't know that he can without revealing the name of the woman involved," Elisabeth said.

Emily's face paled. *The woman must be prominent indeed to elicit such a reaction.*

The clock on the mantle chimed the hour. Emily jumped up, alarmed. "I have to get back to the Honey House. I'll be late for work."

It sounded strange to Elisabeth for Emily to talk about what she did the same way she herself would speak of her secretarial position. "Thank you for trusting me enough to confide in me," she said as she escorted Emily to the front door.

"I know you'll think of something, Miss Wade. Or Mr. Strong will." The girl headed off for her evening's employment.

Elisabeth wasn't so sure of that. In fact, she was sure she'd never be able to discuss the topic with Titus Strong. No, she'd have to find another way.

CHAPTER 38

THE NEXT DAY—Wednesday it was—Titus and Elisabeth took their places at the defense table once again. He'd noticed the secretary seemed... tentative... as if there were something on her mind. But when he'd asked her at the office, she'd said there wasn't.

Once the prosecutor arrived, and Katie Sullivan was brought over from the jail, the judge gaveled the session to order. "Mr. Strong, are you ready to proceed with your cross-examination of Mr. Stevens?"

"I am, your honor."

Titus called Fred Stevens to the witness stand and reminded him he was still under oath.

"Mr. Stevens," Titus began, "please tell the court where you are employed."

Stevens looked befuddled for a moment. When he furrowed his brow, Titus became aware of his high forehead, and remembered noting it during the argument at the Seaview Hotel. Stevens looked at the prosecutor for reassurance, but Edgar Garner was whispering with his clerk and paid no attention to the witness. "I work at the salvage yard."

"That would be the *Payne* Salvage Yard, would it not?" Strong emphasized "Payne" to make sure those present understood the importance of this fact.

"Yes." Stevens swallowed hard. "May I have a glass of water?"

The judge ordered the clerk of the court to pour a glass of water from a nearby pitcher and bring it to Stevens. He drank half the glass before he indicated he was ready to continue.

"Do any of the other witnesses at this hearing work at Payne Salvage Yard?"

This time, Stevens's eyes went to Tom Hinkle as he answered. "Why Tom Hinkle, of course. Everyone knows that. He said that before, didn't he?"

He had, but Titus wanted Stevens to remind the judge of that fact. It was more effective when a witness did that, rather than the defense attorney. "Did Tom Hinkle have any relationship to Nate Cooper?"

"Relationship?"

"Let me rephrase that. Were you present when Tom Hinkle had a conversation with Nate Cooper one night at the salvage yard?"

Stevens's eyes widened. "I might have been."

"You might have been? Don't you remember a night last month when Tom Hinkle was at the salvage yard and Nate Cooper came by?"

Stevens's voice rasped when he answered. "I do." He cleared

his throat.

"What was Mr. Hinkle doing at the salvage yard?"

The hands of the witness flexed, curling tightly, then uncurling, and finally coming to rest on his thighs. "Well, you see, we don't make much at the yard. Tom's got a sick kid."

His eyes went to Hinkle again, and Titus followed his gaze. Hinkle was sitting ramrod straight in his seat, his eyes unblinking as he stared straight ahead.

"Sometimes, when they bring in some salvage cargo that can be easily turned into cash, Tom takes a load out in a wheelbarrow at night after the yard closes." He was still staring at Hinkle, his eyes pleading for forgiveness.

"And did Nate Cooper observe one of these occasions?"

"Yes."

"Were you present on that occasion?"

"I was."

"Please tell the court what happened."

"Cooper knew Mr. Payne would be angry if he found out about Tom taking the goods. Tom might lose his job. Or worse. Old Nate, he threatened to go to Mr. Payne unless Tom gave him a cut of the profits each time he took something."

"Did Mr. Hinkle agree to that arrangement?"

"He did." This time he looked at Strong with pleading in his eyes. "You can't blame him for wanting to take care of his kid."

Titus ignored the last sentence. Or tried to. He'd save his sympathies for outside the courtroom. "So Mr. Cooper was blackmailing Mr. Hinkle."

"That's right." Stevens looked crushed.

"Let's go back to the night of the argument between Mrs. Sullivan and Mr. Cooper at the Seaview Hotel." He paused a moment to let Stevens get oriented to the change in topic. "Were you present when that argument occurred?"

"I was. Me and Tom stayed at the hotel that night. We shared a room. You couldn't help but hear the noise if you were trying to sleep."

"Did you see the derringer?"

"I did."

"Where was it?"

Stevens pointed at Katie Sullivan. "She had it in her hand pointed at Nate."

"Did you see Mrs. Sullivan drop the gun?"

Stevens nodded.

"Please answer aloud for the clerk," the judge admonished.

"I saw Mrs. Sullivan drop the gun."

"Did you see the derringer after Mrs. Sullivan dropped it?"

Stevens licked his lips. "I did."

"Where was it?"

"Tom Hinkle brought it into our room."

There were several gasps from the spectators and the judge gaveled them to silence.

"Are you saying that Tom Hinkle was in possession of the gun after Mrs. Sullivan argued with Nate Cooper in the hallway of the second floor of the Seaview Hotel?"

"That's what I'm saying."

Titus picked up the derringer from the evidence table and showed it to Fred Stevens. "Is this the gun Tom Hinkle had when he returned to the hotel room you shared?"

"That's it."

Titus returned the derringer to the evidence table. "Was there another occasion on which you saw Tom Hinkle with the derringer that had been dropped by Mrs. Sullivan?"

Stevens picked up his water glass and drank it dry. "Yes."

"When was that?"

"It was the night of the storm. Me and Tom went out to the lighthouse to talk to Nate. Mr. Cooper, that is."

"What did you go to the lighthouse to talk about that night?"

Stevens's breaths came fast and shallow and beads of sweat popped out on his forehead. "This and that."

Titus frowned. He saw he'd have to prompt the witness to get a straight answer from him. "Did you go to talk to Mr. Cooper about the blackmail?"

Stevens seemed to grab onto that like a drowning man clutches a life preserver. He nodded vigorously. "Yes. Yes, that was it. Tom was tired of paying Cooper off every time he stole something from the yard."

The statement didn't ring true, but remembering what he'd told Miss Wade recently, he didn't dare ask another question he didn't know the answer to. "Did they argue?"

"I'd say so." Stevens seemed on firmer ground here. "They was shouting at one another so loudly, if it hadn't been for the storm, you could have heard them in Town Hall."

"Did they do more than shout at one another?"

Again, Stevens looked at Hinkle before answering. "I thought they were going to come to blows, but instead, Tom pulled out the gun and shot Nate Cooper. I can tell you, I was so flabbergasted, I didn't know what to do for a minute."

"Where did Tom Hinkle shoot Nate Cooper?"

"In the shoulder."

"Did he fire the gun a second time?"

"No, sir. Just the once."

"What did he do with the derringer after he shot Nate Cooper?" As soon as the words were out of his mouth, Titus realized he'd broken his own rule. He had no idea what Hinkle had done with the derringer. He'd assumed he'd shot Cooper twice. Given Stevens's testimony, he'd figured Hinkle put the gun in his pocket, maybe came back later to finish the job. But he didn't know that.

"Well, he was just as amazed as I was. I don't think he meant to shoot Nate at all when we went to the lighthouse. He did it on the spur of the moment, you might say. He took one look at that gun and then flung it away like it was burning his hand."

"What happened next?"

"We got out of there in a hurry. Neither one of us wanted to stick around."

"Mr. Hinkle testified that he lit the lighthouse lamp that night. Are you saying the two of you left without doing that?"

"Oh, no. That's right. Tom said he'd better check the light before we left. Right after he did that, we went back to town."

There was something off about Stevens's testimony, but Titus didn't think he was going to get anything more out of him. Except… "Can you explain why the lamp wasn't lit later on?"

"Objection!" Garner shouted.

"Sustained," Judge Dewey ruled.

Titus rephrased the question. "Did you see Tom Hinkle light the lamp?"

"No."

"When you left the lighthouse, was the lamp lit?"

"I can't rightly say. I didn't think to look at it."

"No further questions, your honor."

"Since we're approaching the noon hour, we'll adjourn until two o'clock this afternoon."

CHAPTER 39

As Elisabeth turned to leave the courtroom, she spotted Amanda in the last row of spectators. She must have come in after the testimony had started.

"Shall we go to lunch?" Titus asked her.

She glanced back at Amanda before answering him. "If you don't mind, I'd like to speak with Miss Cooper. She has no one here to talk with anymore. Perhaps she'll agree to have lunch with me."

Titus stared at Amanda for a moment, then turned his attention back to Elisabeth. "We'll have lunch another day, then. I'll see you at two o'clock."

She watched Titus stride out of the courtroom. Were his shoulders drooping? She didn't want to think about that. In fact, their attraction to one another was one reason she'd packed a sandwich wrapped in newsprint in her purse. She didn't think lunching regularly with your employer was appropriate for an unmarried young woman.

Amanda wasn't far behind Titus Strong, and Elisabeth hurried to intercept her before she left the building.

"Amanda!" she called out just as her school friend was about to step outside.

Amanda turned, spotted Elisabeth, and stepped to the side to allow the throng to pass her.

Elisabeth hurried to join her. "I've been worried about you, especially when you didn't show up at the hearing yesterday."

Amanda's eyes glittered behind the veil. Her eyes were the only feature Elisabeth could discern. Oh, there was a little bump where her nose was, but you couldn't actually see her nose. Even the sound of a sniffle was muffled because of the material covering her face. "It's upsetting to listen to the witnesses talk about my father's death."

"Why not stay away then?"

Amanda shook her head. "I have to know what they're saying. I have to know what happened to cause his death so soon after I lost my dear mother."

"Would you like to talk about it?"

"I don't think so. I'm hanging on by a thread, and I don't know if I'd be able to come back this afternoon if I started talking about things."

"All right. What about supper this evening? Mr. Kelley promised to drop off some of whatever he caught today. It will probably be bluefish, but perhaps he's been lucky and will bring some striped bass, or even a chunk of swordfish."

"I'd like that," Amanda said wistfully.

"It's settled, then. I'll probably have to go back to the office and type up my notes at the end of the afternoon session. Why don't you come to my house at about 7:00 PM?"

"Are you still living at home?"

"It's my home now," Elisabeth reminded her softly. "I also lost both of my parents."

Amanda squeezed her hand. "We'll have lots to talk about then."

Elisabeth watched Amanda go down the steps to the sidewalk, then turn toward Mayfield Road. She must be going back to where she was staying or one of the tourist restaurants closer to the beach for lunch.

The secretary had other plans. She wasn't used to being cooped up inside all day and thought a lunch in the park would be the perfect thing.

She crossed Griffith Road and walked across the luxurious, green grass toward the Revolutionary War memorial. Three benches spaced equidistant from one another formed a semicircle around it, a place to sit and contemplate long ago relatives who had died for their country's freedom. Elisabeth chose the one farthest away. She didn't face the statue with the plaque at its base, but instead looked out over the water of Boston Harbor. You couldn't quite see the city from here, because there was another peninsula between Shipwreck Point and Boston, but there were usually boats sailing past.

She unwrapped her sandwich—the remainder of the cold mutton on two slices from the loaf of bread she'd sliced last night—and chewed thoughtfully on the first bite. Her life had certainly turned out differently than she'd imagined it would when they were girls. At one time she'd thought she might marry Tim Kelley. They'd grown up together, gone to school together, and he came from a respectable family. Oh, not as respectable—meaning rich—as her parents might hope for her, but the Kelleys earned an honest living, unlike many in Whitby, and were steady. Elisabeth had no doubt that she and Tim could make a very nice life together. They'd raise a brood of happy, boisterous boys and cultured girls, and host dinner parties for their friends. Having known one another all their lives, they were comfortable in one another's company.

But there had been no spark between them. Her aunt would have said a couple didn't need a spark to have a successful marriage, but Elisabeth had read all of Jane Austen's books, some of them more than once, and she couldn't help but think that a spark needed to be there. At least for her.

A seagull landed on the white wooden fence that separated the park from the beach below. The bird eyed her hand, and she broke off a bit of the bread and tossed it toward him.

She'd never expected to feel that spark towards an employer, but she couldn't deny that it was there with Titus Strong. If his behavior was any indication, he'd felt it, too. It would be totally improper for them to have a romantic relationship. Even if they did, suppose it led to marriage? She had to believe that he wouldn't expect his wife to work. She'd waited so long for her independence, to have a job where she felt competent that she could earn a living and make a life for herself, she couldn't imagine giving it up so soon.

Fortunately, Titus Strong was already married. That made things a whole lot simpler. Or a whole lot more complicated.

She'd gone to the library on her lunch hour one day and perused the Boston papers, looking for information on her new boss. Elisabeth knew there would be plenty about the recent case that had brought him so much notoriety. She hadn't expected to find an article in the gossip columns about him attending a charity fundraising ball with his wife.

The seagull hopped across the grass and cocked his head up at her. All of a sudden, the mutton wasn't setting well in her stomach. She took the mutton from the remainder of the crusts, wrapped it up in the newsprint again, and broke up the bread for the bird. As soon as she tossed it on the grass, a dozen of his brothers and sisters joined the first bird, and they started cawing and squawking as they tried to chase the competition off so they could have the treat for themselves.

Elisabeth rose from the bench, brushed the crumbs off her skirt, and headed back to the courthouse. She passed a trash barrel on her way and dropped the mutton into it. She imagined her fantasies of a romance with Titus Strong dropping into the trash with it.

CHAPTER 40

"Redirect, your honor?" Edgar Garner asked once the afternoon session was called to order.

"Will Fred Stevens please take the witness stand." As soon as the witness had resumed his seat, Judge Dewey said, "Go ahead, Mr. Garner."

"Mr. Stevens, you testified that Mr. Hinkle shot Nate Cooper once. Is that correct?"

"Yes, sir."

"Where did the bullet enter Mr. Cooper's body?"

"In the shoulder. 'Twarn't hard to miss, what with the blood on his jacket."

"And then Mr. Hinkle divested himself of the derringer?"

"If you mean did he throw it away, he sure did."

"Was Mr. Cooper breathing the last you saw him?"

Fred Stevens frowned. "I'm pretty sure he was." He didn't sound confident.

Garner tried again. "Could you see his chest rising and falling as he took a breath and let it out?"

The wrinkles on Stevens's forehead flattened out, and he answered with assurance. "I could. Yes, I could see him breathing." When he spoke, he sounded amazed that he'd forgotten such a simple thing.

"Was there a large amount of blood on Mr. Cooper's jacket?"

"Naw. Spot couldn't have been more than this big." Stevens made a circle with his thumb and forefinger.

"Thank you, Mr. Stevens."

"Re-cross, Mr. Strong?" the judge asked Titus.

Titus wished he had a question he could ask to discredit the testimony of the thug, but he didn't. "No, your honor."

"In light of this new evidence, I'd like to recall Tom Hinkle," Mr. Garner said.

Hinkle and Stevens swapped places. As they passed one another, Tom Hinkle gave Fred Stevens an evil look.

"Mr. Hinkle, you've heard the testimony given today by Mr. Stevens?"

"Yes." He spat out the word.

"I'd like to ask you some of the same questions you answered earlier."

"I figured you would," Hinkle muttered under his breath.

"What was that?" Garner asked.

"Nothing."

"After the fight between Mrs. Sullivan and Mr. Cooper at the Seaview Hotel, did you pick up Mrs. Sullivan's derringer?"

"I did." He kind of folded in on himself as he pushed one shoulder forward and turned his head away from Garner. His voice sounded sulky.

"Why did you pick it up?"

"I couldn't see a good gun going to waste, even if it was a lady's weapon."

A few of the spectators laughed.

"Did you keep the derringer?"

"I did. Stuck it in my pocket and forgot about it."

"But you didn't forget about it when later on you went to confront Nate Cooper about blackmailing you, did you?"

"I sort of did. I'd taken to carrying it around it my pocket. It was so small, I hardly noticed it was there."

"Tell us what happened in the lighthouse keeper's cottage the night of July second."

"It was the way Fred Stevens said it happened. We went out there to make Nate quit taking a cut of everything I… had to sell." The way he said it, the words didn't quite ring true. It was almost as if Garner had fed him the reason and Hinkle had latched onto it. "He'd been drinking, like he usually was, and he got belligerent. He started threatening me." Hinkle's face darkened. "I don't take too kindly to being threatened. Before I knew it, I pulled the derringer out of my pocket and shot him."

"How many times did you shoot him?"

"Just the once."

"Do you know whether there was one bullet or two in the derringer when you fired it?"

"There was two. I checked it before I put it in my pocket at the hotel." He grinned at Katie Sullivan. "I needed to know whether Mrs. Sullivan was serious about shooting Nate, or was threatening him with an unloaded gun. She was serious all right."

The Case of the Mysterious Madam

"Objection!" Strong said as he leaped to his feet. "Mr. Hinkle could have no way of knowing Mrs. Sullivan's state of mind."

"Sustained."

Garner continued. "So there was still one bullet left in the derringer when you last saw it?"

"Had to be. I only shot it the one time."

"What happened after you shot Nate Cooper?"

"He fell to the ground. I didn't think such a tiny hole could cause that. Maybe it didn't. Maybe the drink caught up with him." He shrugged.

"Was Mr. Cooper alive when you left the lighthouse?"

"He was. I swear to God, he was." His lower lip was trembling. He licked his lips to hide it.

"No further questions."

"Recross, your honor?" Strong requested. He waited a brief moment for a nod from the judge.

"Mr. Hinkle, you stated there was still one bullet left in the derringer the last time you saw it."

"That's right."

"When did you last see it?"

Hinkle wrinkled his forehead. "I guess that was right before I threw it on the floor."

"So you left the derringer in the keeper's cottage?"

"Yes."

"Did you lock the door to the keeper's cottage before you left?"

"No, sir. I don't have a key."

"So anyone could have entered the cottage, found the derringer, and shot Nate Cooper a second time?"

Hinkle nodded. "Yes, sir. Anyone could have." He stared at Katie Sullivan. "Including Mrs. Sullivan."

"Including Mrs. Sullivan," Titus agreed. But he couldn't let that be the last thing the judge heard. "Including almost anyone who was in Whitby that evening."

"I suppose so," Hinkle said.

"No further questions, your honor."

CHAPTER 41

A LUNCH PAIL was sitting on Elisabeth's front porch when she rode her bicycle up to the house. She got off the bike and went to pick it up. When she saw the ice that filled it all the way to the top, she smiled. Joe Kelley had kept his promise of leaving her a meal from his catch today.

She wheeled the bicycle around to the back of the house, parked it in the woodshed, and put the pail in the icebox before taking Daisy out back for her nightly exercise. She didn't let the terrier play as long tonight as she usually did since she was expecting Amanda for supper.

She had just turned the swordfish steak in the frying pan when she heard a knock. Elisabeth hurried to open the front door. Amanda Cooper, dressed in the same clothes she'd worn to the hearing today, stood on her porch.

"Come in, Amanda." As soon as her friend had stepped inside, Elisabeth said, "Why don't you take off your hat and veil? You'll need to take them off to eat anyway."

"All right." Amanda reached up and removed a hatpin, then took the hat off. The veil lifted from her face, revealing careworn features and a pasty complexion, so different from what her face had looked like when the two of them had spent summers on the beach.

Elisabeth took the hat and placed it on a hook on the coatrack just inside the door. "Come into the kitchen while I finish cooking dinner."

Daisy's ears perked up, and she lifted her head as the two women entered the kitchen. She got to her feet and came over to greet the new arrival.

"I see you still have Daisy." Amanda bent and let the dog sniff her hands, then scratched the terrier behind the ears.

"Yes." Elisabeth smiled, but the smile soon faded from her face. "I'm not sure for how much longer. She's getting old."

Satisfied that the stranger was a friend, not a foe, Daisy went back to her corner and lay down again.

Elisabeth caught a whiff of roses as Amanda's skirts swished behind her. It smelled so lovely, she thought she might start wearing a scent herself. "You're still wearing rosewater. What kind is it?"

"Oh, I make it myself from the roses in my garden."

"How clever of you." Elisabeth checked the swordfish, then opened the oven and pulled out a pan of biscuits. As she transferred the biscuits to a basket lined with a clean linen towel, she heard a sniffle. She quickly looked at Amanda, who gave her an apologetic smile.

"Sorry. It's not that I'm so clever. It's more of a necessity. I'm destitute, Elisabeth." She hung her head.

The Case of the Mysterious Madam

"That's nothing to be ashamed of. It happens to the best of us." As she herself well knew. Mr. Kelley had started leaving fish on her doorstep when he learned she often went a day without eating anything other than what she could grow. She patted Amanda's arm. "Let me serve supper, and we can talk about things as we eat." She placed the swordfish steaks on a platter and picked up a bowl of salad she'd put together from the greens in her garden. She held out the salad. "Would you take this into the dining room for me?"

Amanda nodded and led the way, having been in this house dozens of times before. Elisabeth grabbed the platter of swordfish and the basket of biscuits and followed her. Once they were seated, with portions on their plates, she said, "I'm sorry it isn't more. I tend to eat simply now that my father is gone."

"This will be fine. In fact, it smells delicious. I haven't had fresh swordfish in years. Not since mother and I left Whitby, as a matter of fact." She smiled. "I'd forgotten how delicious it is."

Elisabeth filled her in on what their mutual acquaintances had been doing in recent years. She didn't want to make that smile go away too soon, especially not over a meal. When Amanda reminisced about their younger days, she joined in, and the two of them laughed over childhood misadventures and embarrassing moments as they ate.

Their plates were soon emptied, and together they brought everything back to the kitchen. "Just leave the dishes in the sink," Elisabeth said. "I'll clean up after you go. I don't want to waste any of the time we have together tonight."

"You're so kind," Amanda said. "I'd forgotten how kind the

people of Whitby are."

"Aren't people kind in Richmond?"

"Oh, they are, usually. When you're one of them. Unfortunately, when mother became ill, we could no longer entertain as we once did. Even this sort of dinner party was beyond us." Her eyes became wistful.

"Shall we have coffee in the parlor?" Elisabeth asked. "We can talk more comfortably there."

Amanda nodded.

Once they were seated in the parlor, Elisabeth on the settee and Amanda perched on the edge of a chair, Elisabeth said, "Tell me about your mother."

"Mother was never the same after that final night we spent in Whitby." Amanda raised a hand to her cheek for a moment, contemplating her friend's demeanor.

Elisabeth made an effort to frame her features in a look of concern. It wasn't that the concern wasn't genuine, but Amanda and her mother had left their hometown many years ago. She couldn't imagine that more recent events weren't more important to their story.

Making up her mind, Amanda continued, her voice almost a whisper. "You know the reason we left, don't you?"

"There were rumors, but no one knew for certain."

"My father drank too much."

Nothing new there, thought Elisabeth.

"He was a nasty drunk, particularly toward my mother. If she didn't do whatever he demanded the minute he demanded it, he'd hit her. She was always trying to cover up bruises. There was a time he blackened one of her eyes. She didn't leave the house for almost a month, sending me off to do the shopping and errands instead." Amanda paused while her throat worked, whether from the effort to speak or a dry swallow, Elisabeth wasn't sure. Finally, Amanda raised her chin in defiance and said, "The last night, he hit her with a stick and broke her arm. That was when she knew we had to leave him." Her eyes had grown bright with moisture.

"Even he knew he'd crossed some kind of line then. He dropped the stick, and sat in his chair by the fire, drinking from a bottle of Irish whiskey. Mother had me pack up our things, and as soon as he passed out, we came into town and stayed at one of the boarding houses. Mother knew the woman who ran it, so she opened her door to us when we knocked. She didn't charge us for the night." A tear trickled down her cheek, and she pulled a handkerchief from her pocket to wipe it away.

"That must have been horrible for you."

"It was. I was so ashamed."

"What happened with your mother's arm?"

"She didn't want to go to the doctor in the middle of the night. She thought it would cause too much gossip. She didn't sleep because of the pain. I could hear her moan every once in a while as I tried to get some rest. The first thing in the morning, we took our suitcases with us and knocked on Dr. Porter's door. As soon as he set her arm and put it in a sling, we took the first ferry into Boston so we could take a train to Richmond."

"I wish you had written me. Everyone worried about the two of you when you disappeared. It was obvious something awful had happened to force you to leave. Your father stayed drunk for a week.

"Did things get better once you got to Richmond?"

"In some ways," Amanda said. "We no longer had to worry about my father's drunken rages. But we were always the poor relations, dependent on my grandparents, and later on, my uncle, to provide us with a roof over our head and food for our bellies." She sighed.

"Couldn't you seek some employment in Richmond?" While most women didn't work, things were changing. It was no longer considered scandalous for a young woman to have a job and support herself. Of which Elisabeth herself was proof.

"There was nothing I could do." Amanda's voice was almost a wail. "I hadn't realized how unwell my mother was. She'd always hid her bruises and pain as best she could when we lived here in Whitby. But her insides had been damaged by the constant beatings. She had trouble breathing from ribs that hadn't healed properly after being broken. Her digestion was ruined and her kidneys had permanent damage. There was blood." Amanda refrained from describing more details than that.

"We didn't have the money for proper medical care. We had to make do with what I could do for her. I couldn't leave her because she was so poorly. After she passed, I thought I might go to nursing school. I'd had so much practical experience nursing my mother, it seemed like something I'd be able to do."

"And did you?"

Amanda shook her head. "I couldn't. My grandparents had passed away and left everything to my uncle. He didn't see the use of a woman getting an education. He kept telling me I should fix myself up and find a husband." She waved at her body. "But I've never been attractive to men. My frame is too sturdy, and I haven't been young for a very long time. I don't know where my uncle expected me to get the money to buy a proper wardrobe or have my hair, skin, and nails attended to." Amanda sniffled. "I had to face it. I'd become a drudge. No man will ever want to marry me." She ended her tale with a sob.

Elisabeth wanted to tell her that wasn't true, that she had many fine qualities, and that it was still possible for her to marry and, perhaps, to even have children. But she herself hadn't been successful in that endeavor, and for much the same reasons. Once a woman reached a certain age, there weren't many single men available. Images of Titus Strong and Tim Kelley flashed through her mind, but she quickly banished them. She'd already decided neither one would make a suitable husband for her.

"You really have had a tough time of it," Elisabeth sympathized. She made up her mind to turn the conversation in a more positive direction. "But surely now you can find some way to improve your situation? It's early in the summer, and Whitby has plenty of jobs for those willing to work at them. Perhaps one of the shops on Mayfield Road could use a shopgirl?" She was about to suggest cleaning rooms in one of the hotels as an alternative, but realized Amanda wasn't quite ready for such a significant change in what she perceived as her proper station. "I know it might seem below you, but if you could earn enough money, you might be able to pay for nursing school in a year or so."

"I'd been hoping my father would pay for nursing school. That's why I came back to Whitby."

Ah! An opening to the topic she really wanted to discuss tonight. She'd been wondering how she was going to steer the conversation in that direction. "I thought you told me you came to Whitby because of your father's death?"

Amanda shifted her position in the chair, smoothed her skirts, and crossed her ankles. She pressed her lips together for a moment before saying, "You must have misheard me. I was on the schooner that wrecked just as I testified during the hearing. I took the last of what money I had to purchase my passage here. I thought if I could talk to my father, he'd give me the money."

"But, Amanda, your father didn't have any money. What little he earned as the lighthouse keeper, he spent on drink and…" Elisabeth stopped for a second to think of a polite way to say it. "Other pleasures," she finally came up with.

Amanda looked at her slyly. "Don't you remember the tales of pirate treasure we heard growing up?"

"Of course." She smiled. "What could be more exciting to a group of young people than a mysterious pirate treasure?"

"I think my father found it."

Elisabeth raised her eyebrows as she sat back on the settee. "What makes you think that?"

"He was always talking about it like it was some great secret he had. He even gave me a piece of eight he found on the beach once to prove that it really existed."

"He did?"

Amanda nodded. "I'll show it to you." She opened her purse and rooted around inside for a minute. Then she frowned. "It's not here. I must have taken it out to keep it safe. It's probably in my room at the boarding house. I'll fetch it and show it to you the next time we see one another."

Elisabeth thought it was more likely that she imagined she

had a piece of eight from her father. It would be something a young girl with little hope would cling to. "All right."

She stifled a yawn, and Amanda looked at the clock on the mantle. "Oh, I'm so sorry. You must be exhausted from working all day. I imagine you have to be in to work early tomorrow morning."

Regretfully, Elisabeth agreed. "I do. I'm sorry we can't talk longer. You'll have to come for supper again, perhaps when this case is over."

"I'd like that," Amanda said warmly. The sentiment was sincere if the tone of her voice was any indication.

The two women rose and made their way to the front door. When they stopped in the entryway, Amanda glanced at the basket on the small table beside the door and smiled as she reached in her purse again. "It's so nice to see you haven't given up all the social conventions." After some searching, she pulled out a card case, its edges worn with the years that had passed since it was new. She opened it and put a calling card in the basket.

"I don't think that's been used since I was a schoolgirl," Elisabeth said wistfully. "I should entertain more visitors, but that will be difficult now that I'm working for Mr. Strong."

"Is that a permanent position?" Amanda asked.

"No. As far as I know, he's just taking this one case while he's here. I'll have to find something else when he goes back to Boston." The pang of regret she felt at that statement took her by surprise.

"Then you'll be free to have a regular day and time when you'll be receiving visitors."

Rather than correct Amanda, Elisabeth agreed. "Yes, I

suppose that's true." But she knew she'd have to find another job once she no longer had this one. Perhaps cleaning hotel rooms. She stifled a sigh.

"Thank you again for the lovely dinner," Amanda said. "I haven't had such a pleasant time in years." With that, she passed through the open door and descended the steps to the street.

Being July, there was still enough daylight for her to make her way safely back to where she was staying. Elisabeth was glad she didn't have to worry about her friend, at least not about that. Still, she watched Amanda until she turned onto Mayfield Road and passed out of sight before going back inside.

After she closed the door, she noticed a piece of paper that had slipped beneath the small table. Curious, she picked it up and looked at it. It was a letter to Amanda. She had the urge to take it and chase after her friend, but she realized it would be hard to catch up with her at this point. She'd return it tomorrow when she saw her in the courtroom.

Even as one part of her mind was thinking about that, another was absorbing what was in the letter. She quickly glanced down at the signature and discovered it was signed by Nate Cooper. Seeing that, she couldn't help but read the whole thing.

It was as Amanda had told her. The letter, written in somewhat of a scrawl, was a response to Amanda's request for money. Throughout it, Nate denied that he had any money to help her. In fact, he suggested that if she succeeded in becoming a nurse, she might live with him and help him with his expenses.

Elisabeth was shocked at the man's audacity. But not as shocked as she was when she looked more closely at a spot near the bottom of the page.

CHAPTER 42

IT COULDN'T BE. But then Elisabeth thought of the inconsistencies in Amanda's story about how she came to Whitby, her desperate need for money, the tears at her disappointments.

She also thought of poor Katie Sullivan, held prisoner while the hearing went on, and likely to be held prisoner until after her judgment at trial. Elisabeth now knew for certain that Katie Sullivan was innocent, even though the circumstances of her alibi couldn't be shared with the public at large.

The letter might make her currently bleak future somewhat brighter. She'd have to show it to Mr. Strong first thing in the morning.

But that might be too late. With most of the town, and particularly the judge, assuming Mrs. Sullivan was guilty, the hearing had quickly come near to its end. Tomorrow might be the last day, and there wouldn't be enough time to gather evidence of what Elisabeth now suspected had occurred. No, she had to show Titus Strong the letter tonight.

Barely taking the time to fold the piece of paper before jamming it in her pocket, Elisabeth ran back to the woodshed and rolled her bicycle out into the yard. She hopped on it and pedaled toward town as fast as she could.

"You have company," Owen Campbell said from the other side of the card table.

Titus turned his head to look behind him. His mouth fell open when he saw Elisabeth Wade approaching, her hair loose and windblown, most of it having escaped from the careful chignon she wore during the day. He could hear her breaths coming rapidly as she drew next to him. He closed his mouth, put his poker hand face-down in front of him, and rose from his chair. "Miss Wade. What brings you here tonight?"

Elisabeth's eyes flicked around the table, then around the room, before coming back to him. "I need to talk to you."

One eyebrow involuntarily raised itself as Titus cocked his head. He'd been about to ask if it could wait until the end of the hand, but the earnestness of her expression told him it couldn't. "I'll fold, gentlemen," he said to the card players.

Titus took her arm and guided her to the lobby of the hotel. It was empty this time of night, except for some late arrivals checking in at the reception desk. "Will over there be all right?" he asked, waving his free hand toward a grouping of chairs in the corner farthest from the entrance.

His secretary nodded. Once they were seated, she said, "I told you I was having Amanda Cooper over for supper tonight." She paused to let him respond.

He gave a nod of his head as he wondered about the significance of that fact.

"What I didn't tell you was the reason—other than that I wanted to speak to an old friend, that is." Again a pause, as if she were gathering her thoughts. She took a deep breath. "Amanda had told me a different story as to why she came to Whitby than what she testified to in the courtroom yesterday. She told me she'd come on the train after hearing about her father's death."

She had his attention now. "But she knew I had seen her swimming in the ocean the night of the shipwreck, so she knew that story wouldn't hold water, as it were." He grinned at the metaphor he'd unconsciously come up with.

"That's right. When I asked her about it this evening, she said I must have misheard her the first time. I thought she might be right." Elisabeth pressed her lips together for a moment. "But I knew what she'd told me. I hadn't misheard her at all. That made me wonder why she thought she needed to tell me she'd come to town later than she actually had."

"Did you ask her about that?"

"No. It was only after she left that I became convinced she'd lied. And then something else happened."

Elisabeth quickly recounted her conversation with her friend, emphasizing that Amanda wanted her father to pay for nursing school and living expenses while she attended. "After I saw her out, I noticed she'd dropped this."

Elisabeth reached in her pocket and pulled out a folded piece of paper. She handed it over to him and waited patiently while he examined it.

Titus quickly scanned the letter. His eyes stopped and riveted on the stain at the bottom. "Blood."

She nodded. "Do you think it's possible...?"

"There's no way to tell for sure whose blood this is, but it seems to be a great coincidence that it should appear on a letter from Miss Cooper's father."

"That's what I thought," Elisabeth said.

"Wait here," Titus told her. He got up, crossed the lobby, and stood in the door of the gambling room until he caught Owen Campbell's attention. Once he had it, he beckoned him to come out.

Campbell didn't hesitate as long as Titus had. He immediately put down his cards and strode across the room. "What's up?"

Titus recounted Elisabeth's story as they walked across the lobby to join her. When they reached the secluded corner, he said, "I need you to tell Campbell what the address is of the rooming house where Miss Cooper is staying."

The secretary rattled off the street address. Titus was again impressed with her memory. How could she ever have imagined she'd wrongly remembered what Amanda Cooper told her about her arrival?

"I want you to go to the rooming house tomorrow morning, Owen, and ask the landlady some questions. Based on what she tells you, you may have to make further investigations. But do it quickly, because I don't think the judge will allow the hearing to go on another day.

"If at all possible, bring the landlady back to the courtroom with you. Offer her money if you have to. Bring any other witnesses you find at the boarding house if you think they can help Mrs. Sullivan's case."

"I'll have the information for you by lunchtime." Then Campbell grinned. "I'd have it for you sooner if you'd let me start tonight. 'We never sleep,'" he said, quoting the Pinkerton Detective Agency slogan.

"*You* might not, but I'm sure the good citizens of Whitby do. When they're not up to no good, that is."

"May I return to my poker game?" Campbell asked. "You made me fold a flush."

"I'm sorry, if that's the case. Perhaps you'll do better the next hand. I'll see you tomorrow."

As Campbell returned to Golden Chances, Titus spoke again to Elisabeth. "How did you get here?"

"On my bicycle, of course."

"I don't think it's safe for you to be riding the streets at night by yourself. Let me get you a hansom cab."

"Oh, I couldn't let you do that," she protested. "I'll be fine."

She was either one of the bravest women he'd met or one of the most foolhardy. "I insist. I don't want to take a chance on losing a good secretary."

She sighed, then smiled. "All right."

They retrieved her bicycle from the other side of the hotel and rolled it around to the street side. A number of hansom cabs stood waiting for departing customers wanting to head home.

Titus signaled to the first one in line. The driver initially balked at taking the bicycle, but after Titus paid him in advance, including a rather large tip, he changed his mind. The driver was whistling merrily as he drove off.

He wasn't in the mood to play cards any longer. No, he was

The Case of the Mysterious Madam

too invigorated by the positive news to sit in the gambling room. What he most wanted to do was work out his strategy for tomorrow based on the new information Elisabeth had brought him.

He went up to his room and sat at the desk with a legal pad and pen in front of him making notes.

CHAPTER 43

THE NUMBER OF spectators in the courtroom had dwindled by the fourth day of the hearing. Based on the testimony so far, they probably assumed the verdict was no longer in doubt.

Titus wished he could have ended on a stronger note yesterday, but there wasn't anything he could do about that. The prosecution had brought its witnesses. Now it was his turn.

"The defense calls Miss Emily Hartwell."

The young woman rose from her seat and made her way slowly to the witness stand. Her chin trembled, and her eyes barely blinked. She stumbled over the edge of the raised platform where the witness chair was positioned, and Titus reached out to steady her.

After she was sworn in, Titus began his questioning.

"Miss Hartwell, where were you on the night of July second of this year?"

Her voice quavered as she answered. "I was at—" she stopped suddenly.

He realized she was about to give the business name, which in his preparation he'd suggested she not use. He nodded encouragingly at her.

"I was at home," she answered affirmatively.

"Do you live with others or by yourself?"

"I live with Mrs. Sullivan." Her eyes glanced in Katie's direction.

"Where was Mrs. Sullivan that night?"

"She stayed home. It was terribly stormy out. She said she was going to work on the accounts in her room."

"When did she go in her room?"

"Right after supper."

"Did she stay in her room all evening?"

"No, sir. She came out at about ten o'clock to make herself a cup of tea."

"So you can truthfully say that she never left the house?"

"No, sir." Emily stopped for a minute and looked confused. "I mean, yes, sir. I'm telling the truth. She never left the house. Is that what you mean?"

"It is, indeed, Emily." Titus paused. He had nothing else to ask the girl. He knew she was lying, but he was hoping Owen Campbell would soon come back with further information. And a better witness. "No further questions."

"Mr. Garner?" the judge said.

Titus went back to his chair.

Elisabeth Wade leaned over and whispered, "Why did you call poor Emily to the stand? She's terrified."

"I'm stalling for time," Titus said as softly as he could. He frowned and shuffled through his notes. He was stalling there, too. He didn't want Miss Wade to ask him any more questions. He felt guilty enough about subjecting Emily to Garner's cross-examination.

"Miss Hartwell," Garner said in a loud voice. Emily flinched at the sound of it. "You said you were 'at home' on the evening of July second?"

"Yes, sir, I was," Emily replied meekly.

"I believe the place where you live has a name," Garner pressed. Emily nodded. "Can you please tell the court what that name is?"

"The Honey House," Emily rasped.

"Could you repeat that a little louder," Garner said.

"The Honey House," she said again. There were sniggers from the remaining spectators.

"I believe the Honey House is a place of business. Is that true?"

"Yes, sir."

"And what kind of business is done at the Honey House?" Every time Garner repeated the name, he spoke it slightly louder and with more emphasis than the other words he said.

"We entertain gentlemen." Emily glanced at Katie Sullivan, who was looking at him as if she was tempted to strangle him.

At the sound of more laughter, the judge banged his gavel. "This is the last warning I'll give the spectators. Any more laughing or disruption of any kind, and I'll clear the courtroom."

"Were *you* entertaining any gentlemen that evening?"

"There weren't many that came that night because of the storm."

"Please answer the question, Miss Hartwell. Did you entertain any gentlemen that night?"

"I did, sir."

"At what time did you do this 'entertaining'?"

"It was about nine-thirty that I took one to my room." She froze as she realized what she was saying.

"And how long did the gentleman remain in your room?"

"I'm not sure, sir. We don't charge by the hour."

Someone stifled a chuckle.

"Was it more than ten minutes?"

"I think so, sir."

"More than fifteen?" When Emily nodded, he asked, "More than twenty?"

"It could have been."

"Do you think it might have been thirty minutes?"

"I'm not really sure, sir."

"What time did you say Mrs. Sullivan came out of her room to make a cup of tea?"

For a minute, Emily looked confused by the question. Then she said slowly, "Ten o'clock."

"If you were in your room, how could you have seen Mrs. Sullivan come out of hers?"

"Maybe the gentleman was only in my room for twenty minutes."

Garner glowered at her as he added a note of sarcasm to his voice. "Or maybe he was in your room for thirty or forty minutes."

Emily sat dumb, her eyes darting around the room as if looking for someone to save her. Titus squeezed his eyes shut. This was all his fault.

"Let me ask you one more question, Miss Hartwell. Were you telling the truth when you testified that Mrs. Sullivan made a cup of tea at ten o'clock on the evening of July second?"

The poor girl shook her head, then cast her eyes down. "No, sir." She raised her head, "But I know Mrs. Sullivan didn't kill Nate Cooper. She couldn't have."

"And why is that?" Garner asked.

Emily looked at Elisabeth Wade, who gave an almost imperceptible shake of her head. Emily returned her gaze to Edgar Garner, and then, almost as if she were pleading, said, "Because she's not that kind of person. She wouldn't kill anyone."

Strong's stomach was twisted into knots. He doubted he'd be able to eat anything during the recess for lunch that the judge had just called. He thought he'd left behind the courtroom tactics he'd used in Boston, but apparently a leopard doesn't change its spots that easily. Elisabeth was glaring at him.

Not only that, Campbell hadn't shown up with the landlady or any other witnesses. He was certain the judge wouldn't grant him a continuance if he didn't have a witness for the afternoon session by the time the judge called it to order.

"I'm going to put Miss Hartwell in a hansom cab," he told his secretary. She gave him a curt nod. Just as he was about to ask her to join him for lunch so he could explain himself, Owen Campbell charged through the door, a portly woman in a black dress and lace shawl waddling behind him. Titus breathed a sigh of relief as the detective reached him.

"Mr. Strong, this is Mrs. Esther Dawson. Mrs. Dawson, Titus Strong. Mrs. Dawson owns a rooming house in the middle of Whitby."

Miss Wade looked back and forth between Titus and Campbell, with a glance toward the landlady. When he saw her face clear, he knew she'd figured out why he'd had to call Emily Hartwell to the witness stand. "Miss Wade, would you please escort Mrs. Dawson to a place where the two of you can eat lunch?"

She nodded at him. "Please come with me, Mrs. Dawson. I know a hotel that has a lovely dining room where we can get an excellent meal."

Titus was sure the last was for himself, a form of payback for not including her in his plans. She knew he would cover the cost of the meal. In fact, she'd probably charge it to his room bill. He deserved it.

"Come along, Campbell. Let's see Miss Hartwell off and then have some lunch ourselves."

CHAPTER 44

"I CALL ESTHER Dawson to the stand," Titus Strong boomed.

The portly woman tottered to the witness chair. Elisabeth Wade had told him she'd been so nervous, she'd barely tasted the extravagant luncheon set before her an hour ago. Before the landlady crossed the bar dividing the spectator seats from the trial area, Amanda Cooper rose from her seat and rushed toward the door.

Titus caught Owen Campbell's eye, and Campbell got up to follow her.

"Mrs. Dawson," Strong began, "do you own a rooming house in the town of Whitby?"

The poor woman was wringing her hands in her lap. "I do."

"Is Amanda Cooper one of the persons currently residing at that rooming house?"

"Yes, she is."

"Was she residing there on the night of July second of this

year?"

"Yes."

Titus's eyes were drawn to the back of the room as the hinges of the door leading into the courtroom squeaked. Owen Campbell stepped through, holding Amanda Cooper's elbow firmly as he escorted her back inside.

Once Campbell and his prisoner were seated, Titus resumed with more confidence. "What happened on that night?"

Mrs. Dawson cleared her throat. "There was the storm, of course. And the shipwreck. It was an awful storm, something we're more likely to see in late summer, a hurricane, or a nor'easter in the winter. I was surprised Miss Cooper ventured out in it. The rest of my guests had gathered in the parlor where they could comfort one another."

"Are you saying Miss Cooper was staying with you before the schooner wrecked off the coast on the night of July second?"

Now that she'd gotten started, Mrs. Dawson's nerves had calmed down. She placed her hands on the railing that surrounded the witness chair and leaned forward in her eagerness. "Oh my, yes. She arrived the day before carrying her suitcase. She said she'd had to get off the schooner at Falmouth because the captain told her they wouldn't be able to make port at Whitby because of the weather coming in. She took the train to Quincy, then took a cab to my house."

"How did she know to come to your house?"

"Why, she'd written a letter two weeks before, asking for a room. The letter said she'd lived in Whitby while she was young and remembered my house as clean and well-maintained." Mrs. Dawson preened as she recited those words.

"You said Miss Cooper went out the night of the storm."

"Yes, that's right."

"About what time did she go out?"

"It was quite late, about nine-thirty I'd say."

"And what time did she return?"

"It was after midnight. I looked at the grandfather clock in the hall when I went to open the door. I'd been roused from my bed by her fists pounding loud enough to wake the dead and wondered who would be out in that weather at that time of night. Being sleepy, I'd forgotten Miss Cooper had gone out earlier."

"What was her appearance when she returned?"

"Why, she was drenched from head to toe! I told her to stand in the vestibule while I fetched a blanket to wrap around her. I didn't want her tracking water all through the house, you know. She did, anyway. After I helped her to her room, I went back and saw there were wet footsteps down the hall."

"What about in the vestibule?"

"Oh, my! There was a big puddle of water where she'd stood. I got some towels and a mop and bucket to clean it up."

"Was there anything unusual about that water?"

Mrs. Dawson's eyes widened, her pupils two black pinpoints in circles of white, and she nodded.

"Please answer out loud, Mrs. Dawson."

"There certainly was. When I wrung out the mop, the water looked pink. I couldn't imagine why it would be that color, so I blotted what was left of the puddle with a towel. It turned pink where the water touched it. At first, I thought it must be some dye from her dress, but then I remembered her dress was blue, not red or pink."

"Did you think of something else that could have caused

that color?"

"Objection!" Garner leaped to his feet. "Calls for a conclusion on the part of the witness."

"Sustained," Judge Dewey said.

"Did you ask Miss Cooper about the strange color of the water coming from her clothes?"

"Oh, no. I didn't dare."

"Why not?"

Mrs. Dawson looked in Garner's direction, as if afraid he was going to shout at her again. "I thought it was blood."

"Objection!" Garner sounded exasperated.

"Mr. Strong, you will refrain from your well-known tricks in trying to get the witness to answer a question that has already been disallowed."

"I apologize your honor. I meant no disrespect." Strong thought everyone, including himself, knew he was lying, but appearances had to be maintained. "I have no further questions for this witness."

"Mr. Garner?" the judge asked.

"No questions."

"At this point, I wish to re-call Amanda Cooper to the stand," Titus said.

"Call Miss Cooper to the stand," the judge told the court clerk.

"May I remind you that you are still under oath," Titus said.

Amanda Cooper nodded.

"In light of what Mrs. Dawson has testified to, would you like to revise your answer as to when you arrived in Whitby?"

"Mrs. Dawson told the truth. It was exactly as she said,"

Amanda said in a small voice.

"So you didn't come to bury your father when you heard of his death? And you didn't come on the schooner that was wrecked off the coast on the night of July second?"

"No."

"Please tell the court why you decided to come to Whitby after being absent for so many years."

"I was hoping to persuade my father to give me money."

"What did you plan to do with that money?"

"I wanted to go to nursing school. I thought that after caring for my mother for so many years, I had the skills to be a nurse. But I needed the training in order to find employment."

"What led you to believe your father had the money to give you?"

"I thought he had found the pirate treasure, or at least part of it. When I was a little girl, he gave me a silver piece of eight and told me tales about the pirates hiding out in Whitby—only it wasn't called that then."

Titus fingered the piece of eight in his pocket for a few seconds before bringing it out and turning his palm up so Miss Cooper could see it. "Is this the piece of eight he gave you? Or very like it?"

She reached out her hand as if to take it. "Where did you find it? I lost it sometime on the night of the storm. I've been bereft ever since, not only because of its value, but because it's the only thing I had left from my father."

Titus ignored her question. As the defense attorney at the hearing, he couldn't testify. He'd have to draw the information out of his witness. "Where did you go when you left Mrs. Dawson's rooming house on the night of July second?"

Amanda drew her arms back. Her head dropped to her chest. Then she took a deep breath, straightened, and jutted out her chin. "I went out to the lighthouse. I'd tried to see my father during the day, but he wasn't there. I knew he'd return to light the lamp because he wouldn't get paid if he didn't do his duty."

"Did you see your father then?"

"He was there. He was drunk as a skunk, so I knew what he'd been doing all day."

"Did you notice a wound in his shoulder?"

"I did, but he didn't seem to mind it, what with his condition and all. So I decided not to mind it either."

"Did you ask him about lending you money?"

"I asked him." She spat out the words.

"Did he agree to give it to you?"

She shook her head.

"Please state your response for the clerk," Judge Dewey said.

"No." The defiance left her and was replaced by a sob.

"What did you do then?" Titus Strong asked.

Amanda Cooper didn't look at him. She also didn't answer.

Titus tried again. "What did you do then?"

There was still no response.

"Miss Cooper, isn't it true that you were angry with your father before you even arrived at the lighthouse that night?"

"Yes," she whispered.

"And isn't it true that you became enraged when he again refused to give you money to further your education?"

When she didn't answer, he pressed on. "Isn't it true that you picked up the derringer left behind by Thomas Hinkle and shot your father in the chest? Isn't it true there was so much blood, you couldn't help but get it on your clothing? And isn't it true that the pink color of the water that dripped off your dress in Mrs. Dawson's vestibule was caused by your father's blood?"

Amanda Cooper leaned forward and clenched her hands on the arms of her chair. "All right. Yes, I shot my father. After all those years of poverty and pain, to find out he wouldn't help me because he drank every penny he earned made me furious. The bastard deserved to die."

A gasp went up from the spectators at the use of such language by a lady.

Titus Strong ignored the reaction. He addressed the judge. "Your honor, in light of Miss Cooper's confession, I propose that the charges against Katie Sullivan be dropped."

CHAPTER 45

ELISABETH FELT A twinge of jealousy when Katie Sullivan threw her arms around Titus Strong's neck right after Judge Dewey dismissed the murder charge. It was silly, she knew, but feelings were often the opposite of logic. She, Owen Campbell, Mrs. Sullivan, and Titus Strong stood in a circle congratulating one another as the prosecutor and judge left the courtroom, and the spectators did the same.

"I never thought you'd be able to prove me innocent," Mrs. Sullivan said.

"It helped that you weren't guilty." Strong smiled. "Shall we all go to the Seaview Hotel for a celebratory supper?"

"Thank you for the invitation, but I can't wait to get back to the Honey House, catch up with my girls, and sleep in my own bed." Mrs. Sullivan glanced toward Emily, who was waiting at the back of the courtroom.

"Owen?"

"You're paying, I assume?"

"I am. Well, to be honest, Mrs. Sullivan is paying after she gets my bill, but I'll add it to my room charges tonight."

"In that case, I'd be happy to join you," Campbell said.

Elisabeth's heart fluttered in her chest as she waited to see if she was included in the invitation. She didn't want to presume.

"Will you be joining us, Miss Wade?"

His gunmetal blue eyes glittered. She couldn't tell if the sparkle was for her or if it lingered from the elation of his victory. She decided it didn't matter. "I'd love to."

Once they were seated in the restaurant with their appetizers dispatched and replaced by huge platters holding boiled lobsters with corn on the cob and lots of butter, the conversation drifted back to the hearing.

"What led you to believe Amanda Cooper had killed her father?" Campbell asked as he broke open a lobster claw.

Mr. Strong picked up his napkin and wiped his hands before picking up his water glass. "I knew she'd done it as soon as she told me I'd called to her on the night of the storm."

"Called to her?" Campbell asked.

The lawyer summarized what had happened that night, and finished up with, "From the beginning, I was sure she was swimming *out* into the water, not coming in from the ship. Despite her explanation that she'd gotten turned around in the confusion, it appeared to me she was swimming too strongly and with too much determination for her actions to be accidental."

"Amanda was always a strong swimmer," Elisabeth said.

"So you told me." The warmth of Strong's smile flowed to her and through her. In a more businesslike tone, he addressed the detective. "Then Miss Wade invited Miss Cooper to have supper with her and questioned her further about her return to Whitby. She told me about the inconsistencies in the stories Miss Cooper told concerning that event.

"When Mrs. Dawson testified that Amanda Cooper had written her two weeks before to request a room, I remembered the part of a letter in the fireplace at the lighthouse. She must have also written her father, telling him she was taking the schooner to Whitby. That's why he refused to douse the light. Nate Cooper couldn't bear to be the cause of his daughter's death."

Mr. Strong paused for a sip of water. "Amanda didn't have the same aversion. The estranged relationship after she and her mother left, along with her dire financial situation which her father couldn't—or wouldn't—help her with, gave her plenty of motive to kill him."

"I suppose that's true, especially since Tom Hinkle so conveniently left the derringer behind," Campbell said. "Just one more thing…"

"Yes?"

Campbell glanced in Elisabeth's direction, as if looking for her permission. About what, she didn't know until he spoke. "I never understood why you were so eager to defend a bawdy house madam. That kind of case would seem beneath you."

Why was it that men felt embarrassed about discussing certain topics in front of women? It wasn't as if Katie Sullivan's occupation was a secret. Anyone who lived in Whitby for any length of time knew what the Honey House was.

"Beneath me? I don't think so," Strong said. "No, the reason I was so eager to defend her was because everyone else was so eager to declare her guilty. I had a hard time believing no one would come to her defense."

He paused to take another sip of water. "Everyone should have someone who is willing to stand up for them. I decided to be that someone."

The End

Thank You!

Thank you for reading *The Case of the Mysterious Madam!* I hope you enjoyed it. If you liked it, please consider leaving a review or rating on the site where it was purchased. Reviews on Goodreads are always appreciated. Your help in spreading the word is gratefully appreciated and reviews make a huge difference in helping new readers find the series.

Get your free bonus story!

See how Titus and Elisabeth solve "The Case of the Stolen Strongbox." You will also be notified of new releases, giveaways, and pre-release specials by signing up for my newsletter at https://elisemstone.com/newsletter.

Books in the Shipwreck Point Mysteries series:
**The Case of the Mysterious Madam
The Case of the Angry Artist
The Case of the Comely Clairvoyant**

Books in the African Violet Club mystery series:
**True Blue Murder
Blood Red Murder
Royal Purple Murder**

ELISE M. STONE

Double Pink Murder
Ghost White Murder
Holly Green Murder

Books in the Community of Faith mystery series:
Faith, Hope, and Murder
Shadow of Death
A Game of Murder

If you like police procedurals, try my Lacy Davenport Mystery Shorts:
Murder at the Museum
Murder in Stella Mann

About the Author

Elise M. Stone was born and raised in New York, went to college in Michigan, lived in the Boston area for eight years, and ten years ago moved to sunny Tucson, Arizona, where she doesn't have to shovel snow. Her first degree was in psychology, her second in computers. She's worked as a pizza maker, library clerk, waitress, social worker, programmer, and data jockey.

After trying her hand at several kinds of mystery stories, she's discovered she most enjoys those written in the style of the classic books she read in her youth—her youth being a long time ago.

As seemed fitting, the Shipwreck Point Mysteries take place in a time before she, and most of her readers, were born. A simpler time, yet a time filled with intrigue and dark corners of its own.

The Case of the Mysterious Madam is her tenth published book.

I love hearing from readers. You can connect with me at:
Email: elisemstone@gmail.com
Twitter: @EliseMStone
Facebook: www.facebook.com/EliseMStone

Manufactured by Amazon.ca
Bolton, ON

15411925R00152